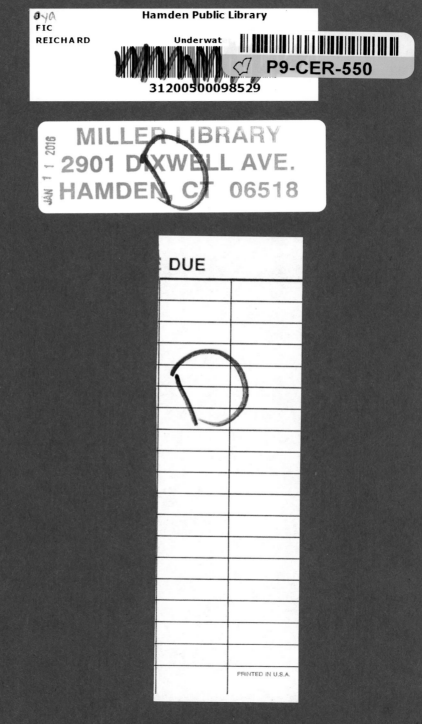

DUE

PRINTED IN U.S.A.

underwater

marisa reichardt

underwater

Farrar Straus Giroux
New York

Farrar Straus Giroux Books for Young Readers
175 Fifth Avenue, New York 10010

Copyright © 2016 by Marisa Reichardt
All rights reserved
Printed in the United States of America
Designed by Andrew Arnold
First edition, 2016
1   3   5   7   9   10   8   6   4   2

fiercereads.com

Library of Congress Cataloging-in-Publication Data

Reichardt, Marisa, author.
    Underwater / Marisa Reichardt. — First edition.
      pages cm
    Summary: Ever since the mass shooting at her California high school,
junior Morgan Grant has become increasingly agoraphobic until even the
idea of stepping outside her door can bring on a panic attack, a situation not
made any easier by the fact that her parents are divorced—but when Evan
moves in next door she finds herself attracted to him and begins to find
herself longing for the life she has been missing.
    ISBN 978-0-374-36886-9 (hardcover)
    ISBN 978-0-374-36887-6 (e-book)
    1. Agoraphobia—Juvenile fiction.   2. Panic disorders—Juvenile
fiction.   3. School shootings—California—Juvenile fiction.   4. Massacre
survivors—Juvenile fiction.   5. Families—Juvenile fiction.   6. California—
Juvenile fiction.   [1. Fear—Fiction.   2. Panic attacks—Fiction.   3. School
shootings—Fiction.   4. Massacre survivors—Fiction.   5. Family life—
California—Fiction.   6. California—Fiction.]   I. Title.

PZ7.1.R45Un 2016
813.6—dc23
[Fic]

                                   2015004184

Our books may be purchased in bulk for promotional, educational,
or business use. Please contact your local bookseller or the Macmillan Corporate
and Premium Sales Department at (800) 221-7945 ext. 5442 or by e-mail at
MacmillanSpecialMarkets@macmillan.com.

For Jon and Kai
my home

u n d e r w a t e r

chapter one

I just moved. Not from one town to another, but from one end of the couch to the other end. I don't usually sit on this side, but I'm trying to listen in on the apartment next door. I'm rather particular about where I sit because I like things to be to the left of me. I need to be able to see what's there.

The walls of our two-bedroom apartment are thin and covered in the standard off-white paint of a rental unit, but I still can't make out the words on the other side. I can only decipher the pitch of the voices.

One is high.

One is low.

Girl.

Boy.

And then I hear feet hitting the linoleum floor and the noise of the screen door as it slaps open followed by the double bang of it shutting back into place.

Someone knocks on my door. Their knuckles thrum against the flimsy wood, and the echo of it rings hollow through my apartment.

Yes, I can open the door. But I can't cross the threshold. That's my rule: *Nothing will ever hurt me if I don't cross the threshold.*

I press my shoulder against the door and grab hold of the knob. "Who is it?"

"Evan."

"I don't know you."

"No kidding." He laughs. "I just moved in next door."

I peek through the peephole. It offers up a long, distorted version of whoever is out there. It's not the best view, but I can tell his hands are empty. That's good.

Even though Evan will eventually segue from new person to neighbor, I'm not eager to get the introduction ball rolling. This kind of attitude is exactly what guarantees that, by the end of the month, Evan will think of me as the weird chick with the frizzy hair who never goes outside. I'm pretty sure that's what everyone else in my apartment building thinks of me. They leave every day, and I stay here. They come home, and I'm still here doing the same thing. But right now, Evan doesn't know all of that, so I should probably open the door even though the thought of it makes my hands sweat. I pull it open a crack. A tiny crack.

Whoa.

Evan is cute.

And he looks my age.

The peephole didn't do him justice.

He runs his hand through his hair. It's fluffy and brown with golden sun-bleached tips. His skin is tan, sun-drenched like his hair, and his nose is peeling. He must've moved from the beach. Literally. Like, he had a hut on the sand. Something about the way he smells makes me want to stay near him. He reminds me of things I miss. I breathe him in, relishing the aroma of earth and ocean and bonfire smoke.

4

"Um, hey," he says. "Are you sick or something?"

I consider shutting the door in his face. How can he call me out so fast?

"Why?" I can hear the edge in my voice, the *back-off*ness to my tone. It's enough to make him straighten up and push back on his flip-flopped feet.

"Sorry. It's just—it's Wednesday. Shouldn't you be at school? Are you home sick?"

Of course he meant was I physically sick, like with pneumonia or explosive diarrhea. Not mentally sick.

"Why aren't *you* at school?" I say.

"Because I'm moving in today and starting school tomorrow." He says this like I should get it. "I can't do both at the same time."

I realize I'm not being the most welcoming neighbor. "Sorry," I mumble. "I don't do well with strangers."

"Does the fact that I now live next door make me less of a stranger?"

"Not really."

"Okaaay." He runs his hand through his hair again like he's frustrated. But also like he's trying to understand. It's the same way my mom looked at me on Thanksgiving four months ago when I told her I couldn't take the trash out to the Dumpster anymore.

"What was it you wanted?" I ask.

He shakes his head, and one of those golden-tipped curls comes loose and falls down over his eye. He shoves it back behind his ear. "Is that your car out back with the tarp on it? It says 207 on the space number. That's you, right?"

"Uh-huh."

"Cool, because my mom needs me to unload the U-Haul. I don't want to scratch your car. Can you move it?"

My heart rate speeds up instantly. It pounds through my chest like rain on the roof. Evan can probably hear the fast and furious thump of it. I wipe my palms against my flannel pajama pants and grasp for excuses. I actually feel like I'm stretching up, reaching for apples on a really high branch.

"I can't. I'm sick. I can't leave. I can't move my car."

I can't. I can't. I can't. It's my mantra now.

Evan looks at me. Brow creased. Perplexed. "Wait, I thought you just got mad at me for assuming you were sick. Now you really are sick?"

"Yep." I cough. "Super sick. And it's really contagious. You probably shouldn't get too close."

He scoots back a couple inches. In the courtyard below, the sunlight smashes against the surface of the swimming pool and shoots a reflection at Evan's feet so it looks like he's standing in a puddle. "You don't wanna move your car?"

"I can't."

"But like I said, it's in the way."

"How about if you move it?" Yes, brilliant. *Good job, Morgan.* Being quick on my feet is a skill I'm getting progressively better at as the months pass.

"You want *me* to move your car? You just called me a stranger five seconds ago. What if I steal it and sell it on Craigslist?"

"You won't. Let me get the keys."

I shut the door and grab the keys from the rack my mom hung in the kitchen after one too many mornings of frantically searching the apartment for lost keys. When I crack the door back open, my breath catches again, because he really is cuter than he should be.

Stop it, Morgan.

I hold the keys up to Evan, but when he reaches in to grab them, my body goes on high alert.

I flinch.

I flutter.

I drop the keys at my feet.

He bends over, calm and steady, eyes on mine the whole time, as he reaches past the threshold to grab them.

His fingertips graze my bare toes.

I jump back.

I breathe fast.

He stands up.

He straightens out.

"Hey, is the pool heated?" he asks. "Or am I gonna freeze my face off if I jump in?"

The pool. I try to ignore it. It taunts me. But I can practically feel the cool water sliding through my fingers and down my back as soon as Evan mentions swimming. I imagine him yanking off his shirt and jumping in. Then I try to unimagine it.

"It's warm enough, but it's too short to get a good workout. And too shallow to pull off a flip turn. Plus you have to scoop the leaves out yourself."

"You sound like you know something about swimming. Are you on a team?"

"Not anymore."

"Oh. Why not?"

"Because. Just bring the keys back whenever, okay? Or, if you sell it, bring me the cash."

"I'll get you a good deal." He laughs. "I don't back down too easy."

I shut the door and hope my car will start. My mom takes it out once in a while to keep it running, but it's old. She's actually threatened to sell it. She says we could use the money. I'm pretty sure she's bluffing. For her, selling my car would be the same as giving up. She'd rather hang on to hope.

My mom hopes I'll go back to school when it's time to be a senior.

I do online high school now. Going to my other school got to be too hard. I can't control things out in the real world. Cars turn corners too fast. Doors slam. People appear out of nowhere. It's unpredictable.

I don't like unpredictable.

Home is predictable enough. Until just now when I realized we have new neighbors. And there's a teenager like me next door. Well, not really like me, because I'm pretty sure Evan actually leaves the house. He looks like he surfs and watches bands play at crammed clubs with entrances in backstreet alleys that require secret passwords. He looks like he rides his skateboard in the empty parking lots of places in town that have gone out of business or zooms down steep hills for an adrenaline rush. So not really like me at all.

Because he has a life.

I go to school online and eat tomato soup and a grilled cheese sandwich for lunch every day.

I form an assembly line along the coffee-stained Formica of the kitchen counter just the way my dad taught me. Bread. Butter. Cheese. Piping hot griddle.

I like the sound of the sizzle of the butter as it hits the pan. It's a reminder of how quickly things change. One second you're whole, the next second you've melted.

I like to put extra cheese on my sandwich so it drips out over the sides. That way, I can scoop it up, twirl it around my fingertip, and suck it into my mouth. I also dunk the toasty bread into the soup, sopping up what's left in the bottom of the bowl. I eat on the couch where the TV is in front of me and the closed curtains are behind me. I'm a shut-in. I'm unaware if it's foggy, sunny, cold, or hot outside unless I'm specifically paying attention. Nothing changes inside my living room. I have a television lineup, online school, the same lunch, and scheduled ten a.m. and two p.m. check-in phone calls from my mom every weekday.

My psychologist visits twice a week.

Her name is Brenda.

She has a hard edge and soft eyes.

She has tattoos that snake up and down her arms until they

get lost underneath the sleeves or the collar of whatever shirt she's wearing.

She comes on Tuesdays and Thursdays after lunch.

At one p.m.

She'll be here tomorrow.

We'll sit on the couch and she'll make me turn off the TV.

I hate that.

Sometimes Brenda forces me to say things that make me cry. But usually, talking to her calms me down. She also checks up on my medicine to be sure I have enough emergency pills. I need them sometimes. On bad days. Brenda can't prescribe them for me because she's not that kind of doctor. She's a psychologist. My regular doctor gave me the prescription after he talked to Brenda.

Today feels different because Evan is next door.

I can hear the *bang bang* of him hammering nails into the wall. I can hear the *thump thump* of him bounding up the stairs. I can hear the *slap slap* of his screen door as he goes in and out, back and forth, up and down the stairs.

Evan is next door. He smells like the ocean.

This runs through my head for the rest of the day. It's what I hear as I sop up soup and sift through soap operas.

I assume he'll bring my keys back when he's done hauling things inside. But when hours pass and he doesn't return, I wonder if maybe he did sell my car. Or at least moved it someplace far away. That would almost be a relief.

But, eventually, there is a knock at my door.

"Who is it?" I ask, as if anyone else ever comes by unannounced.

"Me again. I have your keys."

I flick on the porch light because the evening shadows have set in and I want to be able to see him better. He's a bit sweatier for wear, but his hair is still fluffy and curly and falling into his face in a way that makes me avoid eye contact. He dangles my Pacific Palms High School key chain out in front of him.

"Sorry it took so long, but I put her back where she belongs," he says. "That Bel Air is a classic. How'd you end up with such a sweet ride?"

"It was my grandpa's."

I know nothing about cars. I only know things about this particular matador-red Bel Air because my grandpa told them to me one million times so I could commit the words to memory.

"What year is it?"

"A fifty-seven."

"Your grandpa must've been one cool dude."

"He was." I smile and shut the door.

Evan knocks again. He knocks loud and long. I open the door because I can't not notice him. There's something pulling me closer to the threshold, and I can feel it. There's a tingle in my big toe. I look down and see I've practically got one foot out the door. I yank it back inside, stunned that I even tried.

We stand. We stare.

"Why'd you shut the door like that?" he asks.

Thankfully, my little brother comes soaring through the courtyard right then. His arms are spread out wide like an airplane. His mouth makes the sputtering noises of the engine, and his lips spritz spit into the sky. My mom comes in behind him in

11

dirty hospital scrubs. Her hair is knotted, sloppy, on the top of her head, and my brother's superhero backpack strains against one of her shoulders. She's not a nurse. She does the gross stuff. From Monday through Friday, she mops up blood and puke from hospital corridors. And some nights, like tonight, she comes home balancing a pizza box from Penzoni's on her hip as she struggles to open our mailbox to fish out the pile of bills inside.

My brother takes the stairs to our front door two at a time. He stops short at Evan's feet. His arms fall flat at his sides and some spittle stalls, then sucks back between his lips—*zzzzzip*—as he eyes Evan with kindergarten suspicion.

"Who are you?"

"I'm Evan."

"Evan who?"

Evan laughs. "Uh, Evan Kokua."

Evan tosses out some sort of secret handshake, bumping his fist against Ben's in a way that sends my little brother into spasms of laughter.

"Are you a superhero?" Ben asks.

Evan shoots my brother a grin that lights up the otherwise dingy wraparound balcony outside our front door, then leans down to look him in the eye. "If I am, I'll never tell."

"Awesome!"

Ben pushes past me and through the front door. I rock backward then forward, but manage to stay inside.

And then my mom shuffles up the stairs, hands the pizza box over to me, and looks at Evan. "Half cheese, half pepperoni.

I know it's not very original, but you're welcome to join us, Superman."

She brushes past him to get inside.

Evan shifts forward, ready to make the crossing into our tiny apartment, but he stops midstride over the threshold when he looks at me. My eyes must be bugging out of my face, because he falls back into place on the other side of the door, feet firmly planted on our welcome mat.

"Nah, I better not. I've gotta nail a bookshelf to the wall. Earthquakes."

He shrugs. We all shrug.

California earthquakes. We're all waiting for them. We're all waiting for things to happen that might never come—things that, if they do come, might not be as bad as the things that have already occurred.

"I'm Carol," my mom says, shoving her hand past me to grip Evan's. They shake. He smiles.

"It's nice to meet you, Carol. I'm Evan. My mom and I just moved here from Hawaii. You'll meet her, I'm sure."

My mom throws her arms out on each side of her, accidentally thwacking the hanging planter with the dying fern in it hard enough to send it swaying under the porch light. "Welcome to Paradise Manor, Evan. Ain't it grand?"

"Yeah," I say. "I bet you didn't realize paradise has a view of the Dumpster and no AC."

Evan lets out a genuine laugh that shakes something loose deep inside of me. I like genuine laughter in the same way I like the warm sun on my face, but I haven't heard or felt either of those things in a long time.

"Well, good night, then," my mom says as she slips all the way inside. "You'll have to swing by for pizza some other time. Right, Morgan?" It's not a question. It's an expectation. It's a request to hurry up and have a life again.

"Um, right," I say, rolling the knotted string of my daytime pajama pants between my fingertips. I stand at the door staring at Evan. "Sorry. My mom's kind of embarrassing."

"Not really. She just tells it like it is. It's not like we don't know where we are. It's not like we don't know we're living the lyrics to a bad country song." He fakes strumming a guitar.

Something about Evan makes me want to be brave, so I fasten a fake guitar strap across my own shoulder and strum the strings at my waist.

"She lives in a rundowwwwwn building on the outskirts of towwwwwwn," I croon in an over-the-top country twang.

"Not bad," he says as he backs away from the door, nodding. "Not bad at all. I'm gonna have to write some music to go along with that. Right after I learn to play the guitar."

The idea of us making music together is so ludicrous that it makes me laugh.

Evan grins at me. "You have a good laugh. Like when you hand one out, you mean it. My cousin was like that."

The compliment throws me off-kilter, and I play it back in my head to be sure I heard him right. "Well, your cousin must've been one cool dude."

He smiles halfheartedly. "Yeah. I think you would've liked him." He shrugs his shoulders. "Well, I hope you feel better. My mom swears by soup. Do you have any?"

That makes me laugh again.

"What?"

"That was just really funny in a way you don't even know."

"Oh, well, then I'm glad I could make you laugh. Again."

"Me too."

I'm still laughing as I say goodbye and shut the door behind me. It's a sound that echoes inside and outside of me, and it stops my mom in her tracks when I turn to face her. She stands dead still in the center of the kitchen and looks at me, a smile creeping across her face. It's quick. There and gone. And then she pulls a slice of pizza from the box and slaps it down on my brother's plate.

"You eating?" she asks me.

I nod and pull myself onto my stool at the kitchen counter. The stool where my mom and Ben are to the left of me because they know the drill.

"Evan seems nice. Did you talk for long?" my mom asks. She's fishing.

"Long enough."

"I'm not sure it was long enough for him. He wanted to stay for dinner."

"He shoulda stayed," Ben says. "He's cool."

"Yep, too cool for me, I think." I grab a slice of pizza and turn to my brother. "So who'd you play with at school? I want to hear all about it."

Ben launches into a story about recess. He tells me about how they played Farm and all the kids were different animals and he got to be the farmer.

"That's the best part because then you get to pretend to feed all the people." He laughs, then shakes his head trying to knock his mistake loose. "I mean, the animals."

He keeps talking, animated and stuttering with excitement. I listen to the sound of his voice. And even though the sides of his mouth are covered in tomato sauce and he smells like kickball sweat and playground dirt, I pull him into me and kiss the top of his messy head of hair.

"I love you," I tell him. "You know that, right?"

"Yeah, yeah, yeah," he says through a mouthful of pizza. "I love you, too."

chapter two

My emergency pills are in an amber prescription bottle on the second shelf of the medicine cabinet. I look at them every morning and hope today isn't a day when I'll need to take one. But knowing they are there makes me feel better. I haven't needed an emergency pill for almost two months. Since Valentine's Day. That was a bad day because my dad called. I refused to get on the phone even though he asked to talk to me. That was the last time he tried. But he did talk to my mom, which made her angry. And he talked to Ben, which made him confused. Ben asked my dad when he was coming home, because by then it had been over a year since Ben had seen him. Over a year since he'd returned from his last tour, his fifth one, in Afghanistan. Over a year since my mom had filed for divorce and full custody. Once Ben had gone into another room where he couldn't hear her, my mom told my dad he'd better not even think about showing up at Paradise Manor.

So he didn't.

And he probably never will.

After my mom and Ben have left for work and school, I hold the amber prescription bottle in my hand. I run my thumb over the label that tells Morgan Grant to take one pill as needed.

Not today.

I put it back.

I shut the door.

I hear Evan leave when I'm in my room pulling on a clean pair of pajama pants—I don't see the point of wearing real clothes since I never leave the house. *Slap slap* goes his screen door and *boom boom* go his footsteps on the stairs outside. I pull back my curtains and watch him go.

It's the first week of April, but today will be Evan's first day of school. Everything will be new, but enough of it will be the same. Because it's still high school. And high school doesn't change that much from one place to another. Evan will go to a classroom. He will sit in a desk that faces a whiteboard. A teacher will stand at a podium and tell him things that are supposed to sound smart. Evan will write them down in a notebook covered in graffiti doodles. The girls at school will like him; I'm sure of it. The pretty girls will call dibs and drag him off to the quad at lunchtime to watch them eat apples and sip Diet Coke. I know this because I used to be one of those girls.

I think about these things.

I watch a soap opera.

I eat a grilled cheese sandwich and tomato soup.

I complete two online lessons.

I study Rolle's theorem.

I e-mail an analysis of colors in *The Great Gatsby* to my English teacher.

I wait for Brenda.

I wait for one p.m.

At noon, I know Brenda is coming soon. It is because of this that I feel zingy electricity in my veins. I know she's coming and I have to open the door to let her in.

I have to talk. I have to tell.

Maybe a shower will help.

I duck my head under the hot water and let it soak through to my skull. My hair suctions itself to my ears, locking the noise out. I like being underwater where it's only me. Sounds and the world are far away.

I've spent a lot of time underwater because I used to be on my high school swim team. I swam every weekday, even in the off-season, from three until four thirty p.m., in the twenty-five-yard lanes of the Pacific Palms High School pool. I swam with the same three friends I'd met on youth squad when I was eleven and my dad first received orders to a base near Pacific Palms.

My mom was newly pregnant with Ben so we'd hoped my dad's transfer meant he would be home for a while. But we'd barely gotten settled when he was called up for his third tour in Afghanistan. So he returned to combat and my mom and I committed to making the best of Pacific Palms.

I got close to my swim team friends, and by the time we got to high school, we'd become an inseparable foursome. Chelsea was brilliant and beautiful in that blond SoCal way that made boys stutter when they talked to her. Brianna swam the fifty-yard freestyle faster than any other girl in the history of our high school. And my best friend, Sage, was wise beyond her years, poised to perfection on Model UN and talking about things other sixteen-year-olds didn't even know existed.

I was a little of all of that. But after October fifteenth, after that day, Pacific Palms High School shut down. My friends and I had to go to different schools so construction workers could get busy changing the parts of PPHS that would haunt us forever. The administration split up students based on a set of neighborhood boundaries they'd come up with. The four of us didn't live close enough to go to the same place, so we drifted as things continued to change.

Brianna got a boyfriend.

I started online high school.

Chelsea stopped calling.

And Sage moved away before she was even supposed to start at her new school.

But at our old school, I imagined the bright blue championship banners still hanging from the rungs of the metal fence that ran around the outdoor pool deck. I didn't know if they were still there, but I wanted them to be. Because my name was on one of them. I held a record. I was a long-distance swimmer. I was someone who could go on and on forever, steady and even, then finish hard to pull off the win.

Now my whole life is a race. Every minute leading to the next. Every day feeding into another. It's a constant crossing of the finish line. It's like playing a fast song slow.

Chelsea and Brianna don't understand that. They tried. They'd come over, but we'd only end up sitting and staring at the television.

"Come with us to the party," Brianna would beg. "There are going to be so many cute boys."

"So many," Chelsea would echo.

I'd curl up tighter on the couch, tucking my slippered feet underneath me. "I don't care about cute boys or parties right now. But don't let me stop you from enjoying them."

"It's not the same without you," Chelsea would whine.

Sage would call from her new house on the weekends. More often than not, she'd sound distant and sad and in search of solutions. "So you quit school?" she'd ask. "Is it easier?"

"A little," I'd say.

"Yeah?"

"Yeah."

Brenda knocks her knuckles against my door at 12:57 p.m. I want those three minutes before one p.m. to myself. But she's here. So I breathe deep. I breathe long. And I open the door. Brenda smiles, and I can see the gap between her top two teeth that makes her look like a little kid. I know how old she is because I once asked her to tell me.

"If it really matters, I'm twenty-nine," she said. "But why do you want to know?"

"I just wanted to see if you would tell me."

Today, a long burgundy dreadlock falls into her face, and she tucks it back into the other chunk of dreads she has fastened with an oversize ponytail holder at the nape of her neck. I can see the string of tiny silver loops that line her lobe when she does it. And the peace sign tattoo etched into the skin behind her ear. I pull the door all the way open, and she comes inside.

She sits. She is to the left of me because she knows. She takes out a notebook and a pen. She has pages filled about me. I'm sure she goes back to her office after we meet and types the notes into her computer. She didn't tell me that. I just know. I'd be stupid not to know. Everyone keeps everything on computers.

She pulls the remote from my hand and shuts off the TV with a click.

We stare. We start.

"So. How have the last couple days been for you?"

I tell her about the mundane stuff that happened yesterday and today. Soup. Soap operas. School assignments. And then I tell her about Evan.

"A boy? Your age?" She's intrigued. I can tell by the way she taps her pen against her notebook. "Tell me about him."

"He's tall. And summery."

"Summery? What does 'summery' mean to you?" Her voice is calm, like petting a cat.

And then I tell her about soft sand and crisp ocean water. Of bright blue skies dotted with seagulls and airplanes. Of those same blue skies turning dark and dotted with the moon and stars. I tell her of bonfire smoke and surfboards. Of tank tops and short shorts. Of beach cruiser bicycles and snow cones. Of string bikinis and tan lines. Of parties and promises. Of cold beer and warm kisses.

I tell her all the things I used to be before this. It's not the first time I've told her, but she seems to be listening extra hard today. I think it must be because I sound wistful.

"Do you miss it?" she asks me.

And that makes me cry.

She hands me a tissue, and I sit like a lump on the couch.

"Missing summer is a good thing," she says. "It will be here before you know it. You can be ready for it. You can enjoy it again."

After she's gone, I feel better for a little bit. I don't hate thinking about summer. But then I think too much about other stuff. I curl up into the fetal position, knees tucked into my chest, waiting for the memories to pass.

An hour after that, there's a knock on my door. I'm still curled up, but I've stopped crying. My nose is stuffed up with snot, and I snort it down into my throat. My eyelids are puffy, and the throb of a headache bangs at my temples. I want to be alone. I stay very still and hope whoever is knocking will go away. But they don't. Whoever it is wants me to know they are there.

"Who is it?" I ask through the door.

"Superman."

Even though that makes me smile, I tell Evan I'm not dressed. "I can't open the door."

"Well, get dressed. I'll wait."

So I do. I don't know why, but I do.

I scrub my face. I run a brush through my hair. I dab

deodorant under my armpits. I put on a clean bra and change my stained shirt. I do it all in five minutes flat.

When I crack open the door, Evan's holding some envelopes and a white to-go cup of something. There's a lid on top with three holes poked through it, like the lids of jars Ben uses to collect bugs from the planter at the entrance to Paradise Manor.

"First off, we got some of your mail," Evan says, handing over a credit card bill and some grocery store coupons.

"Feel free to keep them."

He smiles. "Second, I brought you some soup. To make you feel better." I can smell the garlic through the lid when he holds it out to me. "My aunt owns a restaurant. They make good soup."

"I like soup."

"Well, yeah. Doesn't everybody?"

I shrug.

I watch Evan take me in. "Wow, you don't look so good."

"Okay, then." His words hit me hard. I shouldn't have opened the door. I don't need this cute boy from Hawaii to bring me soup and tell me I'm not pretty. There was a time in my life when I knew I was pretty. But I don't feel that way right now.

"Aw, man." He runs his hand through his hair, flustered. "Look, I'm sorry. That came out wrong. That sounded like I think you're ugly or something. Which you're not." He looks down at our welcome mat. "You just look sick. That's all."

Right. Sick. I push my hair back from my face with my free hand, knotting it on top of my head without a ponytail holder.

"It's okay," I say.

"I just meant you seem worse today. So maybe it's one of those things where you have to get worse before you get better."

"Yeah, maybe."

I pull the lid off the soup. A stream of steam hits the air between us. The smell of garlic goes from pleasant to overwhelming.

"I didn't want it to get cold. That's why I needed you to open up," he says.

"Thanks, Superman."

He grins like he's relieved I'm calling him that. I notice dimples digging into his tan cheeks. There's a part of me that wants to nudge my pointer finger into one of them because they're so cute.

"I'm not Superman. Clark Kent, maybe. Not Superman."

"Yeah, okay." I smile.

Evan kicks the front of his flip-flop against the edge of our welcome mat.

"So did you learn to play the guitar yet?" I ask.

"Nope." He laughs. "Did you write any songs?"

"Oh, yeah. Dozens."

"I better pick up the pace then." He grins and those dimples show up again. "But right now, I better go do my homework. This trigonometry class is way ahead of where we were at my old school."

"Trig, huh? So are you a junior?"

"Yeah. You?"

"Same." I don't tell him I'm already in calculus and that math is the one of the few subjects I haven't let slip.

"Well, you need to get well so you can show me around town, okay? I don't know anybody here."

I think about how fun that would've been a year ago. When I was the way I was before. I would've taken him to Clyde's Coffee for frozen hot chocolate. And I would've shown him the strip of beach where the locals hang out and the tourists don't. I would've shown him which hill it was fun to ride down on your bike, and I would've let go of my handlebars and let my arms fly out like wings while the wind whipped past my ears. And on a Saturday night, I would've taken him to a party and leaned into him so his lips would've been close to my ear when he talked. That move always worked. I would've shown him the alcove in the hallway by the auditorium at school where I used to think I could hide and nobody would find me. I would've shown him my world. Now, I can't show him anything but a tiny apartment and a girl who can't walk out the front door.

"I don't get out much. But thanks for the soup. I'm sure it'll taste really good."

Before he can say anything, I shut the door and leave him behind it.

chapter three

Ben loves pancakes. It's our Friday morning ritual, and I wake him up fifteen minutes early to make sure it happens. Today, he climbs onto a stool at the counter and I let him pour the milk and crack an egg into the batter. He stirs and talks. He tells me about kids at school and the words he's learning to spell. He talks about the library and how the section about science is his favorite.

"There's a book about electricity," he says. "And another one about rocks. Rocks are cool. Did you know diamonds can cut glass?"

Pancake mornings with Ben are the best. We eat breakfast and chat until my mom hustles him out the door to drop him off at his before-school program. She runs around the apartment and talks at the same time.

"Don't forget we'll be late tonight. I'm taking Ben to a birthday party." She stops. She stands. She puts her hands on her hips and looks up and down and all around. "Ben, where's the gift?"

"I dunno. You wrapped it."

She runs off to find it. I hand Ben his lunch and ruffle the top of his just-combed hair. "Hey, sneak me a piece of cake if you can. Especially if it's chocolate."

I bend down to zip up his sweatshirt and he plants a wet kiss on my cheek. He grabs me around the neck and holds on tight.

"Rawwwwwr. I'm a dinosaur. I've got you. Rawwwwwr. You can't get away."

I stand up, pretending to struggle under his grasp. He stays put, dangling from my neck like a mess of fat gold chains on a rap star. I swing him around the living room and he laughs. Then I bend down and plant a bunch of kisses on top of his head, tickling him until he loosens his grip and I can slide him back down to the floor. He struggles to stand straight, winded from laughing.

"Have a good day," I tell him. "Don't spend the whole time reading about rocks. Listen to your teacher. Be nice."

"I am nice."

My mom hands Ben the gift so he can carry it to the car, then does one final tug on the bun on top of her head.

"Do something," she tells me. "Even something small."

And they're out the door. And the house is empty. And quiet. I can breathe.

I take a shower. I comb my hair and part it. I put on clean pajama pants and a soft T-shirt from a concert I went to once.

It was at an arena downtown. My boyfriend, Alexios, and I stood in a general admission pit instead of sitting in the assigned seats of the sections above us. Alexios had surprised me with tickets for my sixteenth birthday. It was my favorite band, so I wanted to be in front where I could reach out and touch the stage. Being in front meant people crowded around me, pressing in. Hip to hip. Shoulder to shoulder. Elbow to elbow. Like we were all part of one huge mass. Back then, I didn't mind the crowds. Or the noise. Or the way the ground vibrated underneath me. I wasn't afraid. But Alexios stood behind me anyway. Protective. He was a senior, but he didn't seem too old or too hard to talk to like some senior boys can be. He was my first real boyfriend. And at the concert, his arms were wrapped around my waist. His mouth was behind my ear. He was so much taller than me that nobody dared invade our space. He pushed them off with a simple twist of his shoulder.

Onstage, there was a guy with a bass and a girl on the drums and another girl with a guitar and a microphone. I shouted out all the words because I knew them by heart. I bounced when the songs got faster, and Alexios bounced behind me, still holding on tight.

By the end of the night, we were hot and sweaty and almost in love. We were in love enough that when he told me his parents were out of town for the weekend, I texted my mom to say I was spending the night at Sage's house. But I went home with him instead. We left our jeans and T-shirts in a tangled pile on the floor and climbed into his bed, where he gently pulled me to his mouth by my cheekbones.

We stayed together for six months.

We stayed together until we decided we liked other people. The breakup wasn't ugly or tear-filled. It was simply how it was. It was high school. Alexios was my boyfriend for six months, and then he wasn't.

And now he's in college and I'm in an apartment.

* * *

I spend the rest of the morning watching video lectures for English and calculus, then e-mail in an assignment for US history. After that, I focus on small things. I make my bed and move to the other side of the room to make Ben's bed. We share a room because we have to. We've always had to because we've lived in Paradise Manor since he was born. Ben's bed is to the left of mine. If it weren't, I'd never sleep. I clean the toilet and the mirrors in the bathroom. I pace. I watch. I sit and listen.

My mom and Ben are more than halfway through their days. Evan is, too. I don't know why I think of him, but I do.

I listen to the silence. Then I turn on the TV.

There are news people reporting live from my old high school. I feel my stomach cramp. I might have instant diarrhea.

A pretty news reporter wears a flippy dress and stands by the front office where big chunky metal letters spell out PACIFIC PALMS HIGH SCHOOL on the wall behind her. The reporter talks into a microphone as her hair blows around her face and gets stuck in the hot-pink lipstick on her mouth. She explains that my school is still closed but determined to reopen in the fall. I can hear the wind swish through the microphone. She pulls her hair back and talks about the new language arts building going up on campus. It will be called Finnegan Hall after my English teacher who died there. The building will go where the old one used to be. In between the math building and the auditorium. And the courtyard where Brianna, Chelsea, Sage, and I used to eat lunch will still be right in the middle. The reporter talks about the memorial wall that will be there, too. I fumble for the remote.

Before I can stop it they switch to footage from October fifteenth. They show a line of police cars twisting around the block. They show my classmates filtering out of the school, single file, hands on top of their heads, daring glances over their shoulders at the chaos behind them. My insides clench when I see Chelsea. It's the way I remember her. The news people always show the footage with her in it because she's screaming and crying and looks the most panicked out of everyone.

I can't catch my breath. I feel like Ben is sitting on my chest—the way he does when we are pretending to wrestle. I finally get the remote straight between my fingers. I shut off the TV. I run to the medicine cabinet for my emergency pills. They are there, like a rope tethering me to the world. I need one. For the first time in almost eight weeks, I have to go there.

Twist, thwap, gulp.

I wait.

It's not what I want it to be.

It's not instant.

The zingy electricity is too much. I pace the living room. Back and forth. In front of the window. With the blinds closed. I might be dying.

I'm pretty sure I'm dying.

I don't know what to do, so I call Brenda. She picks up on the second ring. I tell her about what I saw on the news. Chelsea. My school. I tell her how it made me remember. I tell her the building is gone but the memories aren't.

"Seeing it like that is too real," I say. "It makes it all come back."

She tells me to breathe. She tells me I'm okay. She tells me I'm not dying. I close my eyes, take a deep breath, and let it out slowly. She tells me to picture myself in my favorite place, which I say is on a beach towel underneath the hot sun. I miss it. She talks about that place and how I can go there, in my head, on days like this. Her voice is soft, like fuzzy slippers. And when she's done, I can think again.

I tell her I will be okay now.

We hang up. I go to my room. I pick up Ben's stuffed animals from the floor and toss them onto his bed. I lie on my own bed. I stare at the ceiling and think of more good things. I think of Ben on the day he was born, all chubby and pink and bald. We sent pictures and a short video through e-mail to my dad in Afghanistan. He wrote us back saying, *There's my boy*, and told us everyone in his platoon toasted him that day. He was good and proud. He was happy in the way I liked to remember him, because that happiness quickly slipped away when he returned and got even worse when he was deployed again. I think of the way newborn Ben wrapped his tiny fingers around one of mine. I think of sitting next to my mom's hospital bed and rocking him under dim lights while he slept in my arms. I fall asleep to a feeling of a love I never knew until my brother got here.

chapter four

Nighttime makes the darkness last forever. I'm used to being alone during the day, but when my family is gone at night, I feel it. I'm used to snuggling up to Ben before bed and reading him books. We climb between the sheets and he curls into me to turn the pages. I run my fingers along the bigger words, hoping my pointing will help him to learn them. When he drifts off, his head droops underneath my chin and I can smell his apple shampoo. The dirty boy smell has been scrubbed clean. His mouth tilts open as he breathes his toothpaste breath on me. He has dark green pajamas with dinosaurs on them. The top buttons up and has a collar like a fancy shirt someone would wear to work in an office.

Tonight, Ben and my mom are at a birthday party.

Ben is eating pizza.

And cake.

He's playing arcade games.

He will win a prize.

It will be loud and noisy with the chaos of kids.

If I were there, I'd be sweaty. I'd be overwhelmed. I'd want emptiness and I wouldn't be able to find it. I'd have to cup my hands over my ears to block out the noise. Being in the middle of the chaos would make me feel like throwing up. I'd go to the bathroom and grasp the sides of the sink to wait for it to happen.

I'd take deep breaths.

I'd talk to myself in the mirror.

After a while, I'd feel like I could breathe again.

I'd take another deep breath. I'd draw in oxygen like I'd been trapped under an ocean wave and just rose to the surface. It would feel good.

I'd splash cold water from the public bathroom sink on my face. I would think it was gross because the sink wouldn't be very clean. And there would be the faint smell of a dirty diaper coming from the trash can. But I would splash water on my face anyway because of the noise. And the flashing lights. And the screaming kids.

I know these things because I've done these things.

I tried to live in the world after October fifteenth.

I tried and I failed.

After October fifteenth, after that day, we had two weeks of candlelight vigils and celebrations of life instead of classes. Chelsea, Brianna, Sage, and I held hands and cried at every one of them. I told myself we were all hurting in the same way. I told myself I wasn't worse off or different. And then I started at Ocean High School. A school that wasn't mine. I tried to make the best of it. I slung my messenger bag crammed with books and pens and notebooks across my chest and walked through the hallways of my new school like it was no big deal. For three weeks, I pretended the slamming of lockers didn't startle me. And the endless sea of backpacks didn't make me flinch. And the crowded cafeteria didn't make my heart beat too fast. I tried to sit in classrooms and pay attention, but the distraction was there. It was a gnawing feeling in the back of my head.

One day, in the middle of my Spanish class, I watched a girl across the room. She tossed her head back and laughed at something a boy mispronounced. She was pretty and had freckles. He was tall and lanky and had bangs that fell into his face. I gnawed on a pencil and watched them, wondering what it would be like to feel that way again. Then a door slammed across the hallway and it set off a trigger in my body.

I thought I was dying.

I was sweaty. And hot. And sick to my stomach. My heart beat so fast against my chest that I couldn't catch my breath, and I felt like my head might explode because it hurt so much. I stood up, and my teacher stopped writing on the whiteboard to stare at me.

"*Qué pasa*, Morgan?"

"I'm dying." We weren't supposed to speak in English in Spanish class, but I did it anyway.

The blood drained from Señora Gutiérrez's face as her eyes darted to the shut door. She was panicked. I'd said words you weren't allowed to say in a school unless you were serious.

She picked up the phone on her desk and called whoever she was supposed to call in an emergency. People came—an ambulance and medics and police officers and firefighters. And it looked like October fifteenth. It looked like that day. And I'm sure it was very upsetting for a lot of people, because students in

35

my class wrung their hands and peered over their shoulders like they were waiting for the next bad thing to happen.

I was taken away in an ambulance. We went to the hospital where my mom works. She was sweaty when she got to the ER, like she'd run from far away even though it was only from the cancer ward three floors up. She'd run the whole way because that's what moms do when they hear their kids are in the emergency room. When she found me sitting on a bed with the privacy curtain wide open, she hugged me, and I sank into her chest and cried.

My mom went down the hall and around the corner with me, where a radiologist took a CAT scan of my head and an X-ray of my heart. They wanted to make sure I didn't have something majorly wrong with me. I didn't. Not exactly.

My heart was fine.

My brain was fine (sort of).

It turned out I wasn't dying on the outside. I was only dying on the inside, where nobody could see.

After that, we sat in a freezing cold waiting room. I drew in deep breaths of hospital air that I was convinced smelled like blood and bleach. Then the doctor took us into a private room with a door and a window. He gave me some medicine to make me calm. Then he told me I'd had a panic attack.

"But it felt like I was dying," I said.

"It can feel that way," he agreed.

"What can we do?" my mom asked.

"It would be good to find someone for Morgan to talk to."

My mom had to be there the first time I met Brenda because Brenda had to do something called an intake. I think that meant she wanted to talk to both of us to figure out how messed up I was and how often she'd need to meet with me. My mom couldn't afford therapy. I felt guilty for needing it. But my mom was close with some of the doctors at work because she'd had her job for a while. And the doctors at work knew people. And one of them had heard about Brenda. She said Brenda did a certain number of volunteer hours every year and she was willing to use those hours on me because she was particularly interested in helping out military families. The doctor asked Brenda to call my mom. Brenda did. They set up an appointment for the next day in the middle of a bright and sunny afternoon.

I liked Brenda instantly because she was young. And she had tattoos and dreadlocks and all those earrings. It made me trust her. Like she was honest about what she was. Like she didn't have anything to hide.

We sat in cushy chairs in her office. They were deep and green and plush like the carpet underneath them. I think they were supposed to be comfortable, but I felt like I was going to sink into mine and disappear. I asked if I could stand up. My mom and Brenda looked at me funny.

"I can't go to school anymore," I said out loud, my hands fluttering against my thighs. "And I don't want to leave my apartment again."

"Are you sure? Won't you miss your friends?" Brenda asked.

"My friends are all at different schools."

"But you can still see them," my mom said, and then admitted to Brenda that she was worried about the way I seemed to be pushing all my friends away.

"I can't be social right now," I said. "I'm sorry. And I can't go to school. But I did some research. I found an online high school. There's one just for California students, and I can start classes right away."

"I don't know," my mom hedged. "How much is it?"

"It's free. All my classes will transfer, and it's fully accredited."

"It just sounds so extreme," my mom said.

I literally stomped my foot on the ground the way Ben would when he didn't want to jump to me from the edge of the swimming pool when he was three. "I can't go to school. I won't."

Brenda reassured my mom it might be the best thing for me since I'd made the decision myself and had done the research. "Morgan deserves to have some control."

It felt like Brenda understood what I was going through even if I didn't quite understand it. She asked me if maybe I could try to come to her office only twice a week and stay home the rest of the time.

I told her no. I said I couldn't drive. "I can't be in my car. I feel trapped inside of it. I just want to be home where I feel safe."

"Morgan," my mom said, "Dr. Gwynn doesn't make house calls. If you want to work with her, you're going to have to get yourself to her office."

"I *can't*." My voice caught then. I curled into myself. Broken and barely breathing. "What are you not hearing? I can't leave our apartment. I won't."

And then I felt Brenda looking at me. Really looking. Studying silently as I sank deeper. And finally, she sat up straight, her heavy dreadlocks falling over her shoulders, and said, "I'll do it. I want to help."

My mom looked surprised when Brenda said that. To be honest, I was a little surprised, too. Brenda sure was willing to go out of her way for me. She said I had touched her on a personal level, though I didn't know how. My mom said great. And thank you.

So I didn't go to school again. I enrolled in online high school after the Thanksgiving break. The next time I saw Brenda, we sat on the couch in my living room. I told her I needed her to sit to the left of me. She asked me why.

"I need to be able to know what's there. To know it isn't *him*." She said okay and sat down.

I was glad she didn't press me.

I was glad she didn't make me talk about how he was standing to the left of me the last time I saw him.

I didn't want to start with that.

And that's how I've met with Brenda ever since. We started at the end of November, and now it's April. For just over four months, Brenda has been coming to my house to help me get better.

chapter five

My mom and Ben are still at the birthday party when there's a knock on my door. I know exactly who it is. I can picture Evan standing on our welcome mat. I want to see him. I can't help it. Even if all I do is look at him from the other side of the threshold. That's something at least.

I double-check the peephole, then open the door. Evan's right there, his index finger poking through the hole in the middle of a DVD.

"Wanna watch something?" he asks.

It's not like nobody ever comes inside this apartment. My mom and my brother live here. Brenda visits. Chelsea and Brianna used to visit. But Evan is here now. Can I let him in?

I do. I open the door, and he comes inside.

I follow him to the living room and the lopsided couch. I try to scoot past him, to settle into my space before he can sit in it, but he's too fast. He sits down on my end of the couch and waits for me to sit on the other end. I can't.

I stand.

I stare.

I shuffle.

I swear under my breath.

I clench my hands into fists and try to calm down.

"You okay?" he asks, gripping the DVD.

I shake my hands out against the sides of my legs. Fluttery fingers. Nervous hands.

"Morgan?"

"Um, I need to sit there."

"Where?"

"Right there. Exactly where you're sitting." I fidget. I fumble. I freak. "I'm sorry."

"Oh," he says, standing up. "Go ahead."

"I'm sorry," I say again, shielding my eyes with the back of my hand so I don't have to look at him. "I know it sounds incredibly specific."

"It's okay."

He doesn't give me a funny look or anything. Instead he kneels down in front of the DVD player and slides the disc in. He looks over his shoulder to kick a grin in my direction. "Did the soup make you feel better?"

"It was good." And it was. I ate it for dinner the night he gave it to me. But it wasn't the miraculous cure-all Evan had hoped for.

"You smell like coconut," he says, settling onto the opposite end of the couch.

I shrug. My shampoo is coconut-scented. Is it good or bad that I smell this way?

The DVD starts up, and the opening has some music that sounds like summer. It's sweepy and dreamy and goes perfectly with the waves rolling across the screen. The TV fills up with clear blue water crowded with surfers. And then there's a pan-oramic shot of the beach. We watch sand that looks like brown sugar and palm trees slanting sideways into the sun. And then the surfers are there again, the camera zooming in as one of them goes peeling down the front of a wave almost as tall as Paradise Manor. Scribbly writing shows up in the right-hand corner of the screen: *Evan "Da Hapa" Kokua, 17, Pipeline.* There's no mistaking the sun-streaked curls of the boy sitting next to me.

I turn to him, flabbergasted. He looks back at me like, *What?*

"That's you," I say like he might not know.

He glances my way with one eye shut, embarrassed. "I swear I didn't play you this to show off. I haven't even seen it yet."

"What is it? Are you famous? Should I be asking you for an autograph?"

He laughs. "No. It's just a surf video. My friends and I made it. Back home."

"And home is Hawaii."

"Home *was* Hawaii."

"Lucky you." I sigh. "Why would you ever leave?"

Evan shrugs. "Family stuff. A fresh start. My mom wanted to go. There's a list."

I nod and try to think of something I could say to make a move from Hawaii to Pacific Palms, California, seem worth it, but I've got nothing.

"I bet you can't wait to get back," I say, hoping he'll tell me the opposite. Because the truth is I don't want him to leave. Not even from right here, right now, on this cruddy couch.

He smiles at me, and something about it feels so honest and whole, like he sees what I'm wishing. "Hm. Maybe not always."

His reply makes me fumble for another question. "So are you at Ocean High?"

"Yep. You too, right?"

"Sort of."

"You went to PPHS before, right?" he asks me gently, like he's coaxing a feral cat out from behind a Dumpster in a dark alley.

It's not a surprise that he knows about what happened at PPHS. The whole country knows. It was all over TV and the Internet. People grow solemn when what happened at my school comes up in discussion. But Evan's tone almost sounds like Brenda. It makes me worry he knows something more specific about *me*.

"Yes. But I don't like to talk about it," I say.

"Sorry." He tugs at his shirtsleeve, focusing his gaze on the worn edges of it. "I was just thinking maybe you knew my cousin since you were at the same school."

"Probably not." My heart speeds up. My stomach hurts. This subject needs to change. "So this is what you did in Hawaii? Went to the beach? And made surf videos with your friends?"

He looks at me thoughtfully, and I figure he wishes we could keep talking about the other stuff. But then he grins. "Pretty much. I also did ding repairs on surfboards, bussed tables, and threw lemons at rental cars."

"Whoa. That's mean."

"You wouldn't say that if you knew how many kooks visit

Hawaii every year. Millions. What can I say? My friends and I get territorial about our surf spots."

I turn back to the TV, willing myself to get caught up again. There's something so free, so alive, about what Evan and his friends are doing. Another boy slides down the screen on his surfboard, running his fingers through the wall of the wave he's riding. Water skids off his slick skin and into his wake. I can imagine Evan and his posse on the beach, watching their friend from shore, stoked on the moment. And I want to be there. Some tiny part of me wishes I could be part of that day. Out there. Outside. In the sun and the sand and the water, skimming across the screen to nowhere in particular. And thinking about it makes me remember, for a split second, that feeling of just being. And I wonder if I'll ever find it again. Really and truly find it. I twist my gaze from the screen to Evan. He isn't watching his friends surf. He's watching me.

"You love the water as much as I do," he says, nodding at me. "I can tell."

"Mm-hm." My voice drifts. Sentimental. Nostalgic. I haven't swum since the day before October fifteenth.

"Keep the DVD," he says, smiling. "You should have it."

"Really?"

"Yeah. That way, you can watch it whenever you want. And we should definitely go surfing sometime."

When I don't answer, he focuses back on the TV. I watch him watching. He has a faraway look on his face, like he remembers everything about the day that video was made. If I opened my mouth to say it, he'd get it. He'd nod his head and agree. But I don't speak true things like that out loud anymore. The only person I tell things to is Brenda.

And that's one more thing that makes me know that even though Evan and I live next door to each other, we are miles apart.

He will leave his house every day.

He will traipse through the courtyard of our building.

I will watch him go.

He will be a boy living out in the world.

I will be a girl peeking out from behind a curtain.

chapter six

The weekend passes, and when Brenda comes on Tuesday, she says we need a plan for how I can help myself when something triggers a panic attack.

"I'm sorry I called you," I say.

"It's okay." Even though she tells me this, I worry she's at least a little disappointed in me. We've been working for months, and everything she's been teaching me flew right out the window as soon as I saw my school on television. "I wanted to help. But I also want to give you the tools you need to get through those attacks that happen when I'm not available to talk you through them. I want to empower you."

She makes me take out a piece of paper to write down all the things I need to tell myself if it happens again.

> *1. Breathe.*
>
> *2. You are okay.*
>
> *3. You are not dying.*

We've written a list like this before, but it stayed in my notebook. This time Brenda wants me to tear the page free and tape it to the wall. I decide to put it up by the kitchen counter. Anybody can see it. My mom. Ben. Even Evan if I let him inside again. It will be a reminder that the girl who lives here isn't quite right.

I smooth my list out by the photo calendar I made online for my mom for Christmas. April has a picture of Ben blowing bubbles in the courtyard of Paradise Manor. I stare at the bubbles. I stare at my list. Is it really as simple as one, two, three?

"Well, that's done. Let's sit," Brenda says.

We do.

"So. I have to admit, your excitement about meeting Evan the last time we talked made me hopeful you might be ready to try something new. Something simple." She pulls out her notebook and looks at me to make sure I'm following. "But now I'm wondering if it's the right time for that. What do you think?"

"What did you have in mind?"

"Well, there's a mailbox. It's just down the block. I was thinking we could try to walk there sometime. We could send something."

"What? Like a letter?"

"Anything. Even something for your mom. But a letter is a great idea. I can help you with it."

I think of the outdoors and how good fresh air and warm sun used to feel, but there's no way I can make it to the mailbox. "I don't think so."

"Okay. I hear you." She looks at me with her soft eyes. "But please think about it. I'd be right there with you. We could do it together. Baby steps."

"I don't even know who I would write to."

"You can write to anybody."

"Why would someone care if they got a letter from me?"

"I'm sure lots of people would be thrilled. Sage. Your grandmother. Your dad."

"I don't even know where my dad is."

"You could still write him a letter as an exercise."

I think of all the letters I wrote to my dad through his multiple tours in Afghanistan. In middle school, I'd tell him about my collection of first-place ribbons hanging on the knob of my top dresser drawer. I'd tell him about my mom and Ben and chocolate chip cookies. When I was fifteen and high school was new, I'd send him detailed accounts of all the things I was doing and seeing and being. I'd tell him about my swim meets and how I'd clocked the fastest time on my 4x100 freestyle relay team. I'd tell him about my straight A's. I'd tell him about an AP exam. My letters took weeks to get to him. When I was younger, he'd write me back long, detailed accounts of the hot desert and the sandstorms that whipped up around him in the middle of the day. He would tell me he missed me and to give my mom and Ben the biggest hugs I could. But as I got older, I'd be lucky to get back a quick postcard. And eventually, I didn't hear back from him at all. He pulled further and further away.

I definitely took it personally.

He didn't even try to get in touch with me after everything that happened at my school on October fifteenth. And he wasn't even deployed at the time. He was just too far gone. He was drunk and had disappeared.

"War is a mindfuck," he said when he got back from Afghanistan at the end of September a year and a half ago and drank more than he ever had before. As a kid, I remember my dad being a person who'd drink a beer or two at a party or a sporting event or a weekend barbecue. But by last year, he had become a person who constantly reeked of hard liquor. He was spiraling and numbing the pain of whatever flashbacks were giving him nightmares and making him cry out in his sleep. He was short-tempered and made scenes in the courtyard of Paradise Manor. He yelled at me because I hadn't done the dishes or mopped up the water puddle Ben made when I pulled him out of the bath. It was exhausting and embarrassing. By Halloween, after he tossed all our jack-o'-lanterns over the railing in front of our apartment in a drunken rage while everyone in the building watched them smash to pieces below, my mom told my dad they needed to take some time apart. My dad moved in with my uncle Matt six hours down the coast. I'd always liked my uncle, but a part of me was jealous that my ten- and seven-year-old cousins were getting to spend more time with my dad than Ben and I. I assumed he was getting help—he wasn't—and they were getting a better version of him.

Ben asked about our dad a lot, which is probably why my mom invited my dad for Christmas that year.

A last-ditch effort.

He didn't come, of course.

My mom filed for divorce the very next day.

If I wrote my dad a letter, I would definitely have a lot to say. But I'm not sure I want to put that down on paper at the moment.

"Will you at least think about going outside?" Brenda asks when I walk her to the door.

I nod. I think she thinks I'm really going to think about it. Maybe she sees something in me that I don't.

After Brenda's gone, I sit at the computer and scroll through Facebook for the first time in a long time. I see the things my old swim teammates are doing without me. They are at new schools on other swim teams. I didn't even bother to look into joining the team when I transferred to Ocean High after October fifteenth. It's like I had some innate understanding that I wouldn't last there until swim season. And now the people I used to swim with have made other friends. Better friends. They have smiles on their faces that make them look like they're not afraid to keep living. I wonder if it's a lie. I wonder if deep down inside they feel something other than what they're saying.

Like Sage.

After the vigils and before she would've switched schools, Sage moved to Montana with her parents and younger sister. They had family there. Her move made it easier for me to push her away even though the last time I talked to her, she was suffering, too.

"Today was a bad day," she murmured, confiding in me the way one best friend should be able to confide in the other. "I kept seeing my classroom and that boy who fell over on the desk in front of me. Did I tell you about him? His eyes just rolled right up into his head. Don't you see it all the time, too?"

"Can we not talk about it?" I hated when Sage did this. I was trying to block October fifteenth from my head. Her graphic details made that impossible.

"But nobody here gets it. I need you because you were there. You understand."

Her voice was whiny and emphatic, but I couldn't be the one to be there for Sage. I was two weeks in at a new school I hated and barely keeping myself together. Her suffering was too much a reminder of my own. Plus, there were things about October fifteenth that I couldn't tell her, so talking to her made me feel terrible. I felt guilty knowing so many people from my school were sad. Angry. Depressed. It made me wish I'd been better at keeping my eyes open.

"If this is all you want to talk about, I can't call you anymore," I said.

"Well, that's pretty selfish," she huffed.

"I'm sorry."

And that's when I decided that it would just be better if I hid from everyone.

I didn't answer my phone or the door. And eventually, people stopped missing me. That's the great thing about being seventeen. So much can change in only one month. Add two or three to that and it's like you never existed. The Facebook pictures of people I used to know prove it.

I don't know why, but I decide to do a search for Evan while I'm sitting here on Facebook. He's easy to find. My search turns up only one Evan Kokua, and Ewa Beach, Hawaii, is listed as his hometown. I recognize him in his profile picture, his floppy beach hair sticking out all over the place. Golden skin. A wide smile. Big brown almond-shaped eyes. My finger hovers over the mouse, almost ready to click into his "about" section or send a friend request, but I stop myself. I'm not ready to know everything there is to know about Evan. I might find out he's as amazing as I think he is, and it'll only make me wish I could be the same way. I log out of Facebook.

I open a blank document and think I will type out a summary report of the chapter I read for art history. But it doesn't happen. I start typing something else instead. I write to someone I didn't think I'd ever write to. I'm writing to *him*.

It starts like this:

> *Dear Aaron,*
> *Why did you do what you did?*

It goes on from there. I type fast. I have a whole page written in a matter of minutes. I've had so much to say, but nowhere to say it. I tell him about me and who I am now. I tell him what he took away from me even though he doesn't care. I also tell him things I didn't think I would say. I say it all because I have to, even if it will go nowhere.

I print out my letter and sign it. I search through the bottom desk drawer for an envelope. My mom keeps a box of them to send our rent checks to the property management company every month. I fold my letter over twice, shove it into the envelope, and lick it closed. I write his name in the middle. I stare at it. When I see it like that, it feels like a name that doesn't mean anything. *Aaron Tiratore*. It could be anybody.

I don't know his address. I have a school directory. I get it.

I shuffle through the pages, my heart squeezing in my chest whenever I see the name of someone who isn't here anymore. I get to the *T* section. I find him. I write his address underneath his name. I look again. It still doesn't mean as much as I want it to. I delete the letter from the computer and shut it down. I'll work on my art history paper later.

I take the envelope.

I go to my room.

I open the top drawer of my dresser.

I shove the letter underneath my pajamas.

I shut the drawer.

I walk away.

chapter seven

Two weekends have passed since Evan and I watched his surf video. I assume he's found better things to do than visit me. Outside things. Sun, water, and earth things.

Today is Tuesday and Brenda is back. We're supposed to walk to the mailbox. Because of that, I've been up since dawn. Lying in bed. Anxious and alert.

The morning sun shoots through the curtains, lighting up the room just enough for me to see Ben curled up under his sheets. I wonder what it would be like to sleep like him. He twitches in his sleep. He has a smile on his lips. I bet he's dreaming of something good. I'm glad.

He deserves to know good things.

One day I will tell Ben the details of what happened. I will tell him because I love him. He only knows the basics. He knows what happened at my school and that I saw very bad things. He knows I don't leave the house and that I'm afraid. He knows I'm getting help. He knows about Brenda. I hate that he knows these things. I wish I could protect him from knowing. He's only a kid.

The scent from my mom's coffeemaker wafts down the hallway and underneath my door. I get up and jiggle Ben awake.

I go to the bathroom and brush my teeth. I pee. I step on the scale. (I don't know why. I haven't done that since October fifteenth.) A number stares back at me that I've never weighed before. I've gained twelve pounds in six months. It's not like I didn't know. It's not like I didn't see myself in the mirror. It's not like I haven't mentioned it to Brenda. Because that twelve pounds is proof.

Proof that I'm different.

Proof that I eat grilled cheese sandwiches and tomato soup for lunch every day.

Proof that I sit on a couch.

Proof that I go to high school on a computer.

Proof that I stopped swimming.

Proof that I'm not the person I was before.

I used to have long, lean muscles under tanned skin. Now I'm pale white, almost see-through, and I have a ring of fat around my middle that shitty boys on reality TV shows call a muffin top. I used to be able to feel the power in my arms and legs as I sliced through the water of the swimming pool. I used to know the strength of my chest. Of my lungs. Of my heart. I'd probably get winded walking up a flight of stairs now.

I pinch the fat between my fingers because I want to feel it. I want to make myself aware of how far this has gone. I want to look in the mirror and be mad. Disappointed. Maybe I'll get so fat that someday the fire department will have to remove me through my bedroom window with a crane. I'll scratch and scream. I'll cry and say no. Evan will stand in the courtyard and watch. I'll beg for everyone to leave me here, among the junk and the mess that is my life. These are the scenarios I play in my mind when I'm feeling extra disgusted with myself.

I've admitted out loud to Brenda that I don't like the way I look. She tried to reassure me. She said I don't look as bad as I think I do. "You're more different on the inside than the outside," she insisted. "And that's why you're being so hard on yourself."

My mom says I look softer but not unhealthy. "You're not swimming right now. That's all." She says this in that no-nonsense way she has.

Ben says he likes my hair better like this. I've lost the chlorine damage. I call it frizzy. He calls it curly. "You still look like a mermaid," he tells me, squeezing my cheeks between his sticky hands.

I go to my room to get dressed. I pull on jeans. They're tight. I strain to zip the zipper and button the button, but I'm determined to get them on. I need to feel how tight they are. When I'm finally wearing them, I'm instantly uncomfortable. I long for my pajamas. But I want to wear jeans for Brenda. She wants me to go outside.

My mom stops short when she walks into the kitchen. I'm standing at the counter, packing Ben's lunch while he sits on a stool shoveling cereal into his mouth with an oversize spoon.

"You look nice," she says. It's a small thing to say, but it means a lot, maybe even more to her than to me.

She pours a cup of coffee, then sits down on the stool next to Ben to sift through the pile of mail on our counter. I fill reusable containers with carrots, cheese, and apple slices, then arrange them inside Ben's lunch box.

"Too much healthy stuff," Ben says.

"I want you to live forever," I tell him.

Ben gets up and goes to the sink. He dumps out his leftover milk and rinses his cereal bowl and spoon.

Everything about us feels very productive at the moment. We all have a role. Like each of us is an integral part of a team. I like this feeling. It's how we should be all the time. But then Ben and my mom leave, and I'm back to working solo again.

chapter eight

I sit at the computer in my too-tight jeans. I have to do a live session for my US history class before Brenda gets here. I hate live sessions, but my online high school requires that I participate in them twice a month for most of my classes. And by "participate," they mean actually interact with other students and a teacher in a real-time chat session. My non-live lessons are recorded and I can log in any time of day to watch them. At the end of the year, I will have to take finals with a proctor.

I try not to think about that.

I log on to my school website and wait for my teacher to start typing. Since my school only exists online, I sometimes wonder if my teachers are hanging out in their living rooms wearing pajamas the same way I usually do.

There are six other people in my session today. Their names are there in the bottom corner of my screen: Luke, Zhang Min, Amanda, Roberto, Blue, and Victor. I don't know anything about them besides their names. I don't know if they do school online for the reasons most people do—they're famous or super religious or have a medical condition—or because they're like me and too afraid of real school.

My teacher, Mr. Chase, types out a few lines to summarize what we read about the Cold War.

Mr. Chase: *During the Cold War years, we had an America in an elevated state of tension with the Soviet Union. Entire generations were raised with the constant threat of nuclear attack. What do you make of that? How can you compare or contrast it with today's America?*

There is a little red hand icon that we're supposed to click on to chat, like we're raising our hand. There is also a thumbs-up icon if we want to let someone know we liked something they said. And there's another icon of two hands clapping if we're falling all over ourselves about someone's brilliance. I never tap them.

Victor: *It's scarier now.*

Mr. Chase: *How so?*

Zhang Min: *There's actually been an attack. On 9/11.*

Amanda: *Yeah. That makes us similar to the kids from the Cold War generations. We're all waiting for something bad to happen, too.*

Blue: *That's stupid. What a waste of time.*

Mr. Chase: *Blue, I'm all for thoughtful debate here, but remember to be respectful of your fellow students.*

Blue: *Sorry, Mr. Chase. But honestly, what's the point of wasting all your time worrying about something that might never happen?*

Morgan: *Because that's what people do.*

Blue: *No it isn't. I don't. That's what crazy people do.*

Okay. Seriously? What kind of a name is Blue? Is Blue a boy or a girl? I don't even know. But I kind of wish I could smack him or her through the computer right now.

Mr. Chase: *Blue does bring up something interesting. At what point does preparation or overpreparation for disaster become a counterproductive exercise?*

Roberto: *When it becomes all you think about. When you get obsessed.*

Amanda chimes in with a thumbs-up. Blue chimes in with the applause icon. I need an eye-roll icon.

Morgan: *Don't you think it's okay to prepare yourself for the worst-case scenario?*

Blue: *Worst-case scenario is that I'm dead, so why should I even bother worrying about it? There's no point in living to just worry about dying. There's a difference between being prepared and being afraid. You shouldn't stop living your life just because you're scared.*

Victor: *Applause.*

Luke: *Applause.*

Zhang Min: *Applause.*

Amanda: *Thumbs-up.*

And that's pretty much how the rest of the live session goes. It's all hand-clapping and thumbs-ups and Blue being snarky.

I'm so relieved when it's over.

I have become someone who just gets by in school. My grades aren't what they were before. They aren't straight A's worthy of scholarships. Aside from calculus, my grades are just *good enough*. Brenda seems satisfied that I'm still trying. My mom says she's happy I haven't quit. But I know this isn't what she wanted for me. I was supposed to be the first one in our family who got out. I loved English and was great at math. I took AP classes and enthusiastically participated in class discussions and essay contests.

I once wrote my own Canterbury Tale for extra credit. Between my academics and swimming, it was a given that most of my college education would be financed through scholarships. My mom was counting on it. I was supposed to be the one who did something. I was supposed to lead the way for Ben.

But now I'm just good enough.

And sometimes I'm not even that.

I flop down on the couch and think of things while I'm waiting for Brenda. I think of Evan a lot because I can't help it. I think of the smell of him and the way he was after we watched the surf video. That was eleven days ago. I wanted to believe he liked my company. But when the video was over and he stood up from the couch to walk to the front door, I figured I'd either said too much or too little. Because he was leaving instead of staying.

The video was only fifteen minutes long. I wished it had been longer. I wished it had been all night. When we got to my door, he hovered at the threshold. The moon was big and fat and full in the sky behind him. It lit up the whole courtyard. Music seeped out from an open window in the apartment across the way. It was something fitting for a warm night. Something I would've listened to before going to a party last summer. It had a lazy, strummy guitar and syrupy-sweet lyrics. It was the kind of music that would've made me think the night held the promise of something.

Sage, Chelsea, Brianna, and I would pull up to the curb in front of a house by the beach.

The front doors would be open.

There would be music and laughter and a crowd of people spilling out into the yard.

We'd stand on the sidewalk reapplying lip gloss and smoothing out spaghetti-strapped sundresses.

We'd follow one another to the front door, leaving a trail of various fruit-scented body washes behind us.

I'd stop at the stairs.

There would be a boy I knew on the porch.

He would have a beer and a sunburn.

He'd be leaning in a way that made me want to listen.

He would motion me over and we'd talk for hours.

Later, I would kiss him underneath a street lamp.

His tongue would taste like beer and his hair would smell like the handmade waffle cones from the ice-cream shop where he worked.

It would all be so perfect.

And then it would be gone.

Standing at my front door with Evan was nothing like that. It was just a night. There were no streetlamps or friends. There were no promises of anything.

He had pushed back on his heels. "Well, thanks for watching my video."

"Thanks for showing me. It was cool."

I wanted him to stay. Would he think I was crazy if I asked him to do that? *Just say it*, I thought. My mom and Ben would be at the birthday party for a while still. It would be easy to hang out. But I didn't say it. I didn't say a word.

Even though that music was playing, there was a silence between us.

"Do you think you'll be back at school soon?" he asked.

I knew I had to tell him. "I don't really go to school. I do school here. On the computer."

"Whoa. That's so cool."

He didn't get it. He looked at me like I was something special. Like I didn't need school because I was better than that.

The front gate pounded shut, the clash of metal echoing through the courtyard. It made me jump and retreat farther inside. Evan looked down below and held his hand up to wave.

"It's my mom," he told me.

She came up the stairs. She wore a flowy skirt and a blouse that floated out behind her. She was tan. She was pretty. She was tall, but not as tall as Evan. Like him, she looked like she'd just stepped off the sand. But when she got closer, I saw her under the brightness of the porch light. I saw something else. I saw dark circles under her brown eyes and the exhausted slope of her shoulders.

Evan leaned in to hug her, then introduced us when they broke apart.

"Morgan, Janice. Janice, Morgan."

Evan's mom stifled a yawn, then held her hand out to me. When I took it in mine, I could feel the bones through her skin.

"I'm so sorry I haven't come by to introduce myself," she said. "Things have been . . ." She paused, searching for the right word, finally settling on "busy."

I told her I understood even though I didn't. I had no idea

what it was like to be busy anymore. My life before was busy all the time. Every second I lived had something in it. But not now.

"I need a shower," she announced. "I'm glad I finally met the neighbors. Or, well, one of the neighbors."

She ruffled Evan's hair the same way I do to Ben, only she had to stretch up to reach him. He looked embarrassed. And then she headed inside, the screen door slapping shut behind her.

"Well, that's my mom."

"What does she do?"

"Everything." Evan sounded tired just thinking about it. "My aunt's having a rough time, so my mom took over running her restaurant while she works through some things. She knows what to do because their parents owned a diner when they were growing up. But the hours aren't easy. My mom's always there instead of here."

"You must be lonely."

He shrugged his shoulders. "It's okay. I understand why she has to do it. And it's a job. We couldn't exactly move here unless she had one."

I probably could've asked a whole bunch of questions that would've convinced Evan to tell me his whole life story, but I didn't want to sound like Brenda. Sometimes it's nice to know someone without having to talk all the time.

chapter nine

Brenda comes at one p.m. just like she said she would. She always does exactly what she promises. She's wearing leopard-print work-out pants and a sweatshirt. She has on running shoes like she is going to compete in a 5K for rock stars instead of just trying to convince me to walk to the mailbox.

"Nice jeans. Does this mean you're ready?" She says this like she's known I'd go all along.

Of course, I can feel all the things I can't control happening to my body. My erratic heartbeat. My armpit sweat. My stomach cramps. I know Brenda can tell because she puts her hand on my shoulder and squeezes it, anchoring me.

"It's okay. We can start right here," she says.

I look at her standing outside my door like it's no big deal. It seems so simple. Why can't I go? Why can't I just cross the threshold and step outside? I think hard. I can't do it. I turn my back to her to head inside. She grabs my shoulder and urges me back around. There's something about the way she regards me right then. It's in the shift of her hip and the squint in her eyes.

"You're ready for this, you know?" We make eye contact. It's the kind of eye contact that means something. She makes me believe her.

And maybe that's all I need, because before I know it, I've pushed myself through the door. But the physical reaction to what I've done is instantaneous. I'm standing on the welcome mat, but it feels more like I'm standing on the edge of an airplane wing in flight. I wobble, out of control. My senses ramp up times one thousand. The sun is so bright that it makes my eyes water. The air is so fresh that it stings my nostrils. The birds tweet so loud that it hurts my ears. But Brenda still stands there, looking at me, knowing I can do it. So I stay put, feet planted on the ground.

"How are you feeling right now?" she asks.

"Overwhelmed." I'm sugarcoating. The more accurate word is *terrified*.

"You should be proud of yourself. I'm proud of you."

I look at her, and it's obvious she means what she says. I fall to my knees, right on top of our welcome mat, and sob. I rock back and forth, clutching my stomach because I want to be able to shove the feelings back inside. But I can't. I cry, loud and long. Brenda squats down next to me. She puts her hand on my shoulder. I feel it. There's just enough force to let me know she has me and that I won't float away.

"It's okay," she says. "You're okay. It's a big step. You're going to be emotional. But you got outside. I might've overestimated with the mailbox. We'll go slower. Baby steps. Just know that I hear you."

Her voice is soothing. Her words still me. My crying calms. I can catch a breath. It's decided that I won't go farther than this today. But this far is still good.

We finish up our hour on the welcome mat. She asks me if it feels good to be outside.

"I like the smell of the air," I admit. And then we talk about it.

She asks me what I notice. What I hear. What I see. "Does it seem different?"

I try to explain what it feels like to be here. Outside. It's more than visceral. It's emotional, too. I try to put that into words. Brenda says she understands.

She doesn't even write anything down. When I ask her why, she says it's because she doesn't need notes to remember this. She tells me that today was a breakthrough. She says it's literally the first step out the door.

"How did you know I was ready?" I ask when we stand up again.

"I didn't. It was only an idea I had. Something I wanted to try. When I showed up and you were wearing jeans, which is different for you, I was hopeful but still not sure. I was prepared for you to change your mind. But then you turned around to go back inside earlier, and I noticed you had a letter sticking out of your back pocket. And then I knew I was right. Without a doubt."

I stand and stare at Brenda.

"Writing is a powerful thing, Morgan. I don't know who that letter is for, but my guess is that writing it made you feel better. You should keep writing. Putting things down in words might help you to process them."

She sounds really sure. She makes me believe it was a good idea.

After Brenda leaves I go to my room. I put the letter back in my top dresser drawer, saving it for another day.

chapter ten

Brenda was right. It feels good to write things down. I spend the rest of the afternoon on my bed, writing stuff in an old notebook. I write about things I want to remember. Short paragraphs that read like photographs.

I write about the first time I urged Ben underwater for half a second in a swimming pool when he was a year old. I write about the way his eyes bugged out when I pulled him back to the surface. He clung to me and I felt bad for scaring him. The summer after my freshman year, when I began teaching swim lessons at the community pool, I realized I went too fast. There are steps I should've taken to prepare him. Thankfully, by then, Ben swam like a fish. I was relieved I hadn't made him afraid of the water.

I write about the way my mom and I used to drive around to garage sales when her belly was fat and full of Ben and my dad was in Afghanistan. Piece by piece, weekend by weekend, we found everything we needed for a new baby. My dad was excited for Ben to come, even though he wouldn't be there for his birth. When we talked on the phone, he would tell me I was going to be the best big sister in the world.

"The key is to hold the baby so they can hear your heartbeat," he told me. "That's how I used to get you to sleep. And once you fell asleep, it was so peaceful and you were so sweet, I didn't want to put you in your crib. So I'd hold you until I fell asleep, too." He sighed. Wistful. "Sometimes all the way until morning."

I write about what it feels like to tear down the lane of a swimming pool and how all the noise gets blocked out. I write about what it feels like to touch the wall at the end of a race and pop my head up to check my time on the scoreboard. I write about my mom cheering. I write about winning.

I write about people I used to know and how I used to be. When I was a friend of girls. And a girlfriend of boys.

And finally, I write a letter to Evan because I want to. I want to know him. My words are real. I have to say them. Because there are things about me he needs to understand if he's going to know me. And they're things I can't imagine saying to his face. Not yet. Writing is safe. I tell him what happened and what I'm like now. I tell him I stay inside because I'm afraid. I tell him I'm working on it, but I don't know if I'll ever change. I tell him he's the first person I've wanted to know in a very long time. I tell him things that are real and true, and I hope admitting them will make him come back, because the last eleven days of not seeing him have felt like a really long time.

chapter eleven

I decide to deliver my letter to Evan as soon as I'm done writing it. I'm eager to get it to him before I chicken out. I want to be someone Evan might like. Maybe it's selfish to want that because liking me is a lot of work, but I think it's brave, too. I open my front door. I peek out, craning my neck to see his front door. Even standing on my welcome mat, I'm too far to be able to reach his apartment. If I toss my letter over there, I might miss and risk it sailing through the slats of the balcony railing and into the pool. Evan has a welcome mat, too. It says ALOHA on it in rainbow colors. If only I could take a couple steps, I'd be able to stick my letter under it. Or I might even be able to secure it near the handle of the screen door. I visualize this. I breathe. I move my upper body forward, but my feet don't follow. They can't. Being out here alone is different from being out here with Brenda. Evan's apartment is too far away. So I do the only thing I know how to do: I go back inside and lock my front door behind me.

That night, Ben rushes inside, practically plowing my mom down as she pulls her keys from the knob. He's all flushed and panting, with his brown curls sticking to his sweaty head. He unzips his backpack and yanks out a red folder, shaking it in my face.

"Look! I'm in a play!"

He's so excited, and it's hard not to get caught up in it. I high-five him. "That's so cool. What are you going to be?"

He wrinkles up his nose. "I'm a frog. But a really smart one. I know everything."

"Sounds like the perfect role for you."

My mom chuckles as she moves past us and into the kitchen, where she sets two bags of groceries on the counter.

"It's gonna be in the auditorium," Ben continues. "There's a real stage there. They even have one of those spotlight machines. And everyone is invited. Even you. Will you come?"

I try to imagine myself sitting in a dark auditorium packed with people and not being able to keep my eye on all of them at once. The idea makes me feel so sick that I almost wonder if I need an emergency pill. I take a deep breath. I think of my list.

1. Breathe.

2. You are okay.

3. You are not dying.

I brush the hair back from Ben's face and pull his chin up to look at me. "We'll see."

"You're going to come, right? Yeah, I know you're going to come." It's like he's talking himself into believing it. I don't know what to say, so I plant a kiss on his cheek instead of talking. He plops down on the middle of the living room floor to look at his script. "Wanna read all the parts with me?"

His grin is so huge. It's as wide as the whole room. I sit down next to him and pull him into my lap. "Tell me who you want me to be," I say.

"You can be all the parts except for the frog. And the alligator. I want to be the alligator, too. He's crazy." He waves his hands up in the air to indicate *crazy*.

I laugh. "Okay."

When we finish reading, I send Ben next door to deliver my letter to Evan before I change my mind. I wait. My heart thumps. And I cross my fingers.

Ben comes back a little bummed out.

"Nobody's home. But I left it for him."

"Where?"

"By the door."

"Good job. Thank you."

So now I have to wait. And wonder. I picture Evan reading my words. What will he think of them?

An hour later, it's dark and cold outside, but it's cozy and bright in my apartment. I help Ben with his homework and fill up the tub for him with warm water and bubbles. My mom fixes dinner, and we eat together in front of the TV. We watch a cartoon that makes Ben laugh so hard, he snorts.

"Chew your food," my mom says.

I hear Evan and his mom come home while we're eating.

I hear them banging around in the kitchen. I hear the whir of the microwave. I tilt my head toward the wall, trying to make out the sound of something meaningful.

"You okay?" my mom asks.

"Mm-hm."

But she doesn't stop watching me.

I eventually hear the clanging of dishes in the sink next door. And then I don't hear anything at all. Ben falls asleep against my shoulder. My mom picks him up off the couch as his arms droop limply at his sides. She shuffles him off to the bedroom.

I sit in the dark for a few minutes. I want to be alone. But then my mom calls out to me.

"Go to bed, Morgan."

She doesn't like to fall asleep and then have the noise of me brushing my teeth wake her up an hour later.

I peek out of the peephole of our front door on my way to my bedroom. I can't see Evan's front door, of course, but I can tell the porch light isn't on. Everything outside of our apartment is dark. And quiet. It's the kind of silence that hurts.

I stop at the entrance to my mom's room before I turn into mine. She's sitting in bed, reading a romance novel. She buys them from the spin rack at the hospital pharmacy. The cover of her book has a guy with long hair and no shirt kissing the bare shoulder of a lady in a ripped dress on the deck of a pirate ship.

"Mom?"

She sets the book down on her stomach. "Yeah?"

There are things I want to tell her, but she looks so tired. I want to say I went outside today. I want to tell her Brenda was

73

proud of me. But then I think maybe I need that to be something that only belongs to me right now. I don't want to get her hopes up.

"I just wanted to say good night."

She holds her arms out to me, and I cross over and sink into them. She brushes my hair back from my face and kisses the top of my head like I'm Ben's age.

"You okay?" She talks against my hair so her words are kind of muffled.

I nod and hug her tighter. The safe smell of her makes me wish I could stay there all night. Instead, I stand up, kiss her on the cheek, and sneak quietly into my room so I don't wake up Ben.

I slide between my polka-dot sheets. I think of Evan and how my words must've scared him. It seems like he would've come over if he'd been happy to get my letter. This realization makes me question everything Brenda has ever told me. She said lots of people would be thrilled to get a letter from me. But Evan obviously wasn't thrilled. How could I have been so stupid? And what if this isn't the only thing Brenda is wrong about?

chapter twelve

The sound of Evan thumping down the stairs early the next morning wakes me up. He's up before the sun. I peek out from behind the curtains of my bedroom window just as the tail end of his surfboard rounds the corner by the front gate. He's on dawn patrol, getting some surfing in before school starts. All the good surfers in town do that. I know the smell of him without being there. I think of him sitting astride his board, bobbing around in the middle of the ocean, waiting for a wave and missing Hawaii.

My letter definitely scared him.

I picture Ben waving his hands up in the air last night when he said the alligator in his play was crazy. Maybe Evan thinks about me that way. He doesn't want to deal with crazy.

I pack Ben's lunch. I watch him and my mom hustle out the door. My mom's keys jingle as they dangle from her fingertip when she goes. I smile as I watch Ben soar through the courtyard. He trips and almost falls into the pool, but my mom catches him by his elbow just in time. And then they push through the gate, disappearing just like Evan did this morning. Neither of them realizes I'm standing on the welcome mat watching them go.

My day is my day: Schoolwork. Soap operas. Sandwich. Soup.

A little after three p.m., I hear the *thump thump* of Evan

climbing up the stairs. Like a total creeper, I rush to the front door and peer through the peephole, but he's already moved past my welcome mat. I can hear him outside, though, so I move to the window and open the curtain just enough to peek outside without being seen. I catch sight of him as he bends down to pick up something.

He studies it.

I can't tell what he's holding until he stands straight again.

He turns it over in his hand.

My letter.

He didn't see it until now. Ben must've shoved it under the mat. Or it was hidden in the dark. That's what I get for sending a five-year-old to deliver the most important thing I've ever written.

He rips it open.

He backs up against the railing of the balcony in front of my door.

He reads.

I want to know what he's thinking.

I watch him even though I shouldn't.

The look on his face stays put. It doesn't give away anything.

> *Dear Evan,*
>
> *I want to be honest with you, so here's the thing: I'm all messed up. I assume you heard about everything that happened at Pacific Palms last year. Well, I was there. And I saw a lot of things. And I'm guilty of stuff I can't even put into words because I'm still trying to figure*

everything out. I have a psychologist who helps me.
Sometimes I wish someone could erase my memory. Because
it changed me. I don't leave my house anymore. That's why
I go to school online. It's not because I'm a genius; it's
because I'm scared.

But then I met you and I thought we could be friends.
You're the first person in a long time that has made me
want to walk outside my front door. You're the first
person who's made me think I might like to ride a bike
again or go to the beach or swim in a pool. And even if
you think I'm too crazy to bother with, I still have to
thank you because I'm trying now. You've reminded me
of things I miss. And I realize I miss them enough to
want to find them again. I really hope this doesn't scare
you. I hope you want to know me, too.

I could never say these things to your face. I needed to
write them instead of speaking them.

Morgan

I skitter from the curtain to hover behind my front door. I picture Evan reading my letter with his backpack hanging off one of his shoulders. I swear I can hear him breathing. It's been hours. It's been a whole night. And all that time my letter was hidden somewhere he couldn't see. Sometimes the things we are sure of aren't true at all.

I jump when he knocks. I stand still, wanting something I'm afraid to want. He thrums his knuckles against the door again.

"Morgan, open up."

I draw in a breath, let it out, and open the door.

"Why didn't you tell me this before?" he asks.

He's holding my letter between his fingers, and I'm concentrating on the way it looks. Like he's holding my feelings right there in his hand. I think about the way my words are on the page. *I really hope this doesn't scare you.*

"I was afraid to tell you," I say.

"But why?"

"I sound crazy."

"You're not crazy."

"You don't know me."

"Fine. But I'm willing to give you the benefit of the doubt."

I can tell he's speaking as true as the sun shining behind him.

"That's why we're here, too. My cousin . . . he . . ." Evan gets caught on the difficulty of his own words. "We're here because my cousin was one of the ones. He went to your school and, well, you know."

I do know. I know exactly. And the fact that I know makes me sick to my stomach. He tried to bring up his cousin when we watched the surf video and I didn't let him. I cut him off. Maybe that's why he disappeared after that night. He probably thinks I'm heartless.

"Who was your cousin?"

"Connor Wallace. Did you know him?"

Evan is looking at me so hopefully that I wish more than anything I'd known Connor Wallace. I wish he'd been more than just another person I passed in the hallway sometimes. Or took an art class with once. I vaguely remember him sitting at an easel on the other side of the room. He was good. Everybody knew that. He won an art contest with a self-portrait he painted in class. I was terrible. None of my art ended up looking like what I'd pictured in my head when I started. If I concentrate really hard, I can see the family resemblance between Connor and Evan. But Evan is more olive-skinned and beachy than Connor. The Hawaiian half of him shines through.

"I knew who he was, but I didn't *know* him," I say.

"That sucks." He kicks at the welcome mat, disappointed. "I really wanted you to say you knew him."

I scramble to make it better. "We took an art class together once."

He sighs. "I know."

"Yeah, right," I say, laughing off what he said. But I stop when I see the sincere way he's looking at me, his big brown eyes locking on mine, practically pleading.

He runs his hand through his fluffy hair. "God, this is gonna sound so psycho." He takes a breath. "I know who you are."

I take a step back. What does he mean? How much does he know? Does he know the things I don't tell Brenda?

"Connor told me about you, okay? Because he liked you."

"Oh, my god." I feel like my knees might buckle out from under me.

"Sorry. I didn't want to weird you out."

"It's not that." I shuffle. "I feel like a terrible person for not knowing him."

He shrugs. "You can't know everybody."

"But I should've known someone who liked me."

"Nah, he never gave you a clue, I bet." He laughs at that thought, like remembering how good Connor could be at keeping a crush secret is funny. "But he liked you. A lot. Since freshman year. We were tight, and he talked about you all the time. Every summer and spring break when he visited. Every Skype session. He had it bad."

"But how did you know I was the same Morgan?"

"I put it together when I moved your car. I mean, how many girls at your school drive old-school Bel Airs? I figured you had to be the one he'd told me about. And that kind of made me want to know you in real life. Like, you were somehow a part of him. But I should've told you that first day. I'm sorry I didn't."

"Wow." I shake my head, trying to take it all in. "All this time, you've known so much about me. That makes me feel really stupid. Or like I'm a liar or something."

"Not even." He looks down at the ground and up again, studying me thoughtfully. "I guess there was a part of me that wanted to see what you were like on my own. I wanted to see what Connor saw. And I thought of telling you a bunch of times, but whenever I brought up school or my cousin, you shut down." He shrugs. I stand there, feeling like he's pointing out everything wrong about me. Like he sees how messed up I am. "And to be honest, hanging out with you kind of bummed me out. That's why I stopped coming by. Because I thought of how much Connor would've wanted to be me. It almost makes me feel guilty, you know?"

"So hanging out with me is a total bummer?"

"That's not what I said."

"Look, I just told you I never leave my apartment. I get it if you have better things to do than spend time here."

"Well, I don't want to hang out inside all the time, but what's the big deal if we hang out when I'm home anyway?"

"Oh."

"What?"

"Nothing."

"Hanging out with you is better than sitting in my apartment by myself."

He's so matter-of-fact. Like I should get this. Like it's a compliment. But it doesn't feel like one. It feels like I'm only good enough to bother with when there's nothing better to do.

"I sit in my apartment by myself every day," I say.

"But you said you're trying. So it won't be forever, right?"

"You make it sound so easy."

"My aunt, Connor's mom, stays inside a lot. Because she's sad." He sighs. "That's why my mom's running the restaurant. It's her sister. We had to move. We had to help. And since we got here, my aunt is doing better. My mom even got her to come help out with the dinner rush last weekend. So see?"

He looks at me hopefully. Like he's waiting for me to walk right out the door and down the stairs with him because his aunt did it.

"But I'm not like her. I don't stay inside because I'm sad. I stay inside because I'm scared."

"I'm sorry you're scared," he says.

"Please don't pity me."

"I don't." He sounds annoyed that I'd accuse him of that.

"Fine."

He simply smiles. "Okay."

Evan is nice enough. But now I can see he might not be talking to me at all if Connor hadn't liked me. And now that I know that, I wish I could tell him I'd known his cousin so I had something to make knowing me worthwhile. I want to have a story that's heartwarming and original that Evan can carry with him forever. I want him to be able to tell his mom the story so she can tell his aunt. Maybe it would make her day. But the truth is, Connor was someone I had never talked to and never will. And now he's one of the names on the memorial wall.

chapter thirteen

"Do you want to come in?" I ask Evan while he's still standing on my welcome mat with my letter in his hand. "We can do homework."

I step aside and hold the door open all the way. Even if hanging out here is only a matter of convenience for him, it's everything to me.

"Uh, sure." He hoists his backpack onto his shoulder and comes inside. "Wait. You still have homework?"

That makes me laugh. "Of course. Online school is still school. I have to do all the same assignments and stuff."

"How does it work exactly?"

"I have to put in five instructional hours a day, but I can do them whenever I want as long as it's over a twenty-four-hour period. And then I e-mail all my homework and assignments to my teachers."

"Oh. That's actually pretty cool."

I shrug. "It's okay. Are you hungry?" I ask.

"I could eat."

He follows me into the kitchen, and I swing open the door of the fridge. There's not much to be said for what's in there.

"We have strawberries," I tell him. "Or I could make you a grilled cheese sandwich."

"I love grilled cheese."

Evan sits down on a stool at the counter while I form my assembly line. Bread. Butter. Cheese. Piping hot griddle. I could make grilled cheese with my eyes closed. But knowing Evan is watching me makes me nervous.

"I like extra cheese. What about you?"

Evan nods. "Sure."

I slap another slice of cheese onto the bread and turn to face him.

He's really here.

At the kitchen counter.

In my apartment.

Wearing a faded red T-shirt for a surf shop in Haleiwa, Hawaii.

One of his curls comes loose and flops down across his eye. I'm zoned out, watching him as he pushes the curl back behind his ear. Then he jerks his head up and sniffs the air.

"I think it's burning," he says.

I turn around to see smoke billowing up from the bottom half of the sandwich. Seriously? How many grilled cheese sandwiches have I made in my lifetime? He must think I'm a total idiot.

I pull the griddle off the burner.

I dump the charred sandwich in the trash.

I start over.

Bread. Butter. *Extra* cheese. Piping hot griddle.

I promise myself I won't look at Evan this time.

But that's really hard to do.

Because everything about him says *Look at me.*

Plus my words. They're just sitting there on that folded piece of paper in the envelope sitting on the counter next to his elbow. Thankfully the sandwich is sizzling. I can flip it now. I won't watch him.

When I set the grilled cheese and a cup of milk down in front of him, he digs in like he hasn't eaten all day. I can tell it's too hot because he does that thing where he whistles in air to cool off the food that's already in his mouth.

"Don't burn your tongue. Geez."

He laughs and takes a long slug of milk. "Sorry. I'm starving."

"Surfing makes you hungry, I bet." He looks at me weird, and then I realize I shouldn't know he went surfing before school this morning. Or any morning. I was just lurking. I was staring out the window, watching him go.

I stare at him now. I watch him eat because I can.

"You're not hungry?" he asks.

"I'm good."

He takes another bite. "You kind of rule at making grilled cheese."

"I'm okay."

"Why do you do that?"

"Do what?"

"Blow off compliments."

"I don't."

"You kind of do."

"Sorry."

"Don't apologize. Just learn to say thanks."

Evan's eyes dart around the room. They settle where I wish they wouldn't: my list. My heart thumps against my ribs like a marching band. My stomach hurts. I don't want to talk about the letter because writing things down and saying them out loud are very different. And I definitely don't want to talk about my panic attack countdown.

 1. Breathe.

 2. You are okay.

 3. You are not dying.

"What's that?" he asks, gesturing to the piece of paper taped to the wall like it belongs there.

"Just this thing," I say.

He raises his eyebrow at me. He knows that's not the whole story. He shoves a golden-tipped curl behind his ear and looks at me like, *And?*

"It's for emergencies."

He looks at the list again, like he's thinking about it. "That makes sense," he finally says, and finishes off his milk.

When Evan's done eating, he unzips his backpack to fish out his homework. The sound of him riffling around makes me stop in my tracks. I eye the backpack like Ben eyed my mom's pancakes that time she snuck zucchini peelings into the batter. And then Evan looks at me the same way I'm looking at the backpack.

"What?" he says.

I don't look at him. Instead, I twist my neck to try to peer past the half-opened zipper. I'm overcome by the need to know exactly what's inside. And he must know, somehow, in some innate way, because instead of getting accusatory, he forces his backpack all the way open and pulls out the balled-up sweatshirt on top so I can peek inside. It's full of the usual backpack stuff. Folders. A novel. Pens. Math and history textbooks. I nod.

"Thanks," I say.

He tosses the backpack on the floor and grabs a folder and a book. We sit down on the couch. But instead of sitting on the opposite end, he sits down in the middle, right next to me, so our arms touch like it's the most regular thing ever. But it's completely the opposite of the most regular thing ever, because I swear I can sense every tiny thing about him. I'm wearing a tank top, and having my bare skin against his bare skin makes me feel everything. It's like I can even feel the fine hairs of his arm brushing against my own.

He cracks open his US history book, pushing against me when he does it. The weight of his shoulder against mine is too much. I scramble up from the couch, telling him I'll be back in a second. *This is what you wanted*, I remind myself as I stand in front of the mirror in the bathroom and run a brush through my hair. When I return, Evan is fully immersed in his homework. I've calmed down enough to settle back into the space next to him and get to work.

We study quietly, side by side. It's nice to have someone else here. It feels more like real school, even if we aren't sitting in a classroom with a teacher and a whiteboard.

But then Evan starts groaning and erasing things, tearing through notebook paper with what's barely left of the eraser on the top of his pencil. It turns out he really is behind in trigonometry, so I admit I can help him.

"How do you know all this?" he asks after I've walked him through half a dozen homework problems.

I don't like to brag, so I just say I worked hard at it. And I did work hard at math. I used to work hard at everything. I worked so hard that working hard became my whole life. Brenda said that being that way probably led to me having the kind of meltdown I had. She said I had a predisposition for that sort of thing because I was focused and precise. Sometimes positives are negatives. She explained that overachievers sometimes end up like me after something tragic happens. It's a reaction to realizing we can't control everything. I also worry that I'm the way I am because of my dad. Like I inherited something.

"Where's your dad?" I ask Evan. And the way I say it comes out loud, like an accusation. He shifts on the couch, keeping his grip on the folder on his knee.

"He's still in Hawaii. My mom and dad are divorced, in case you were wondering."

"Mine too," I say. "Why didn't you stay with him?"

His jaw clenches in the slightest way. "Not an option."

Okay.

"Have you always lived in Hawaii? I mean, until now."

"Yah, sistah. I da kine, one hundred pah-cent local boy, li' dat!" He elbows me in the ribs, laughing, which makes me laugh, too.

"I have no idea what you just said, but I think you made it clear you're from Hawaii."

"You heard right."

"You must miss it. And your friends. They seemed fun in that surf video."

"They are. We had good times."

"I feel like I know them."

"Yeah?"

"Yeah."

And maybe he thinks fifteen minutes isn't enough to be able to know anything. But in my experience, fifteen minutes can make all the difference. Fifteen minutes can change your whole life.

"Are you going back? After school gets out?" I ask, hoping he says no.

"Not permanently. I have to visit my dad as part of the custody agreement, which is stupid because it's really only about leverage for him." Evan scowls. "But I'll get to see my friends when I go. That's the one good thing about it."

"Does your mom want to go back?"

"No way. My mom's had island fever for years. She met my dad on vacation there a couple years after she graduated from high school and never left. But that didn't work out, obviously. And then it was just a matter of finding the right time to get off Oahu—to get my dad to okay the move, I mean. Since he doesn't want me living with him year-round, here we are."

Yep. Here he is. On my couch. With his arm touching mine.

"Hey," Evan says, nudging his elbow into my side. "Where's your dad?"

"I don't know."

He nods like he gets it. "That sucks."

"Yeah, it kind of does."

After an hour, Evan slams his book shut. He stretches his arms high above his head. His shirt rides up, and his tanned, toned belly peeks out between his shorts and the bottom of his T-shirt. I try not to look, but come on. He reaches across me to grab the remote control from the table and flicks on the TV.

"Cool?" he asks, cocking his head at the set.

"Okay." I could use a break anyway.

He settles deeper into the couch, really getting comfortable. I sit there with my arms flat against my sides, my fingers gripping the edges of the cushion as I watch the TV channels pass by. *Please don't let anything be on the local news. Please don't have a panic attack in front of Evan.*

He changes the channels slowly, pausing on practically every station to see exactly what's showing. It's after five p.m. The news could be anywhere. A reporter could be at my old school, standing in front of that building again. The idea of it makes my scalp sweat. I can smell the hallway at PPHS. I can hear the screams and then the silence.

"Go faster." My words come out like a shout.

"You okay?" Evan asks. He's looking at me in a way that says I can tell him anything. But I can't. I can write about it, yes. I can put things down on a piece of paper, then fold it over twice and

90

stuff it into an envelope for him to read. But I can't talk about it out loud. Not now. Maybe not ever.

"I don't want to watch the news. Can we skip over those channels? Like, immediately?"

Evan punches a number into the remote and, like that, we're way off into the bottom-tier cable channels. My mom doesn't make enough money to afford the really good stuff like HBO.

"Better?" he asks.

"Uh-huh."

"You're sweating."

"I know."

"Should I be worried?"

"Please don't be."

"Okay."

He finally settles on some reality show where everyone is fighting and nobody uses proper grammar. My English teacher from last year would've hated it. *Reality TV is like fingernails on a chalkboard,* she used to tell us.

Now her name is on the memorial wall.

And Finnegan Hall.

Evan drapes his arm on the top of the couch behind me and taps my shoulder with his fingertips. "This show's hilarious." He laughs when some guy loses his grip on a greasy pole he's trying to shimmy up. He slips downward, losing his shorts in the process, and gets eliminated from the competition.

"Okay."

The show ends up being all right. I do laugh a little. And being with Evan calms me down. We sit and watch back-to-back episodes until Evan's mom texts him to say the restaurant is busy and she won't be home until late.

"Looks like I'll be nuking my dinner tonight," he says.

It almost makes me feel bad that my mom and Ben will be home soon. I could ask Evan to stay here for dinner. But if I ask him, he might say no. And I'm not ready for that.

"We'll have to hang out again," Evan says, getting up. "Especially now that I know you're a math genius. I need your skills."

"Oh, I don't know if I'll have time. I get pretty busy staring at this wall and that wall. And counting the tiles on the kitchen floor. Have you seen how small they are? I always lose track somewhere in the hundreds."

He laughs. "You're pretty funny for a girl who never leaves her apartment."

I shrug.

"If anything, I'll be back for the grilled cheese," he says.

"I'll be here."

chapter fourteen

When I walk Evan to the door, he asks me for my phone. "Let me punch my number in. We can text."

I have to explain that I don't have a cell phone anymore. They're too expensive. I paid for my old phone with the money I made teaching swim lessons in the summer.

I don't have a job.

I don't have a phone.

I don't have a life.

I'm weird.

"I don't have a cell. I can't afford it."

Evan tucks a curl behind his ear. "Wait right here," he says, as if I might actually leave to go to the corner store for bubble gum. He heads next door and comes back in minutes.

"You can use this." He hands me an outdated cell phone. "It's my Hawaii number. My mom sweetened the move here by promising me a new phone. My old one's not the greatest, but it's prepaid and just lying around. It's something, right?" He enters his California number into the contacts list. "Text me anytime. For real."

He hauls his backpack onto his shoulder and leaves.

I hover at my doorway and watch him go inside his own apartment. After he's gone, I can feel the smile on my lips. My face feels stretched out, and I have to stifle the laugh that wants to come bursting out of my belly. I run my thumb over the top of the phone and wonder how long I have to wait before I can send him a text without looking like a total stalker.

I must look happy, because when my mom comes home, she notices.

"You're kind of glowing," she says as she dumps her purse on a stool at the counter.

I stand in the kitchen spooning three separate servings of chicken and rice onto plates and turn my head to hide a smile. I want my afternoon with Evan to be something only I know.

"Now she looks like she has a sunburn," Ben says.

"Grab the silverware," I tell him.

I'm restless through dinner and reading to Ben. I'm restless because I want to text Evan. But I wait. I wait until Ben has fallen asleep and I'm settled into the dark of our room between the polka-dot sheets of my bed before I type anything.

Me: *Hi*

The phone instantly vibrates in my hand with a return text. It makes me jump. I didn't think he'd write me back so fast.

Evan: *Who is this?*

Oh, my god. How embarrassing. Did Evan program the wrong number into this phone? Am I texting some random someone somewhere else in Pacific Palms? The phone vibrates again, lighting up the dark with another message before I can type my reply.

Evan: *I'm kidding. Hey, Math Genius.*

That makes me laugh out loud, and I have to stifle my giggle with my shoulder so I don't wake up Ben.

Me: *You suck. That totally freaked me out.*

Evan: *You know it was funny.*

Me: *Ha ha. So thanks for the phone.*

Evan: *I got the feeling u didn't want 2 talk about the letter face 2 face. Maybe this is better? It's like writing.*

Uh-oh. When I wrote that letter, I knew Evan was a couple of miles away at school. He was sitting in a desk or cruising down a hallway in flip-flops and slamming a locker shut. He was far enough away to make the words easy. But right now, with my thumbs hovering over the phone keys, I know he's only next door. It's almost like he can hear me. It's almost like I'm saying it right to him.

But I remind myself that I'm not.

There are a couple of walls between us.

I can do this.

I type out, *Okay.*

Here we go.

Me: *Did my letter weird you out?*

Evan: *Nope.*

Me: *So you want to know everything?*

Evan: *Only if u want 2 tell me.*

I decide I will tell him the parts I can say. The parts I have told Brenda. The things she's written down and saved on her computer.

Me: *The bell rang for first period. I was sitting at my desk.*

I remember my teacher stood at the podium.

I remember everything changed in the middle of first period.

Me: *There was a popping sound in the hallway. And screams. And the door to my classroom swung open.*

I remember the panic.

I remember the smell.

I remember the sounds.

I remember there was another door by the whiteboard that led into another classroom that led into a hallway that led out of the building and into the auditorium.

Evan: *What did you do?*

Me: *I busted through another classroom door and yelled at people to come with me. Not everyone could come.*

I remember we ran.

I remember we scattered.

I remember I left that building and ran into the auditorium.

Me: *I thought people were still following me. But when I got to the auditorium, I was alone. I was worried about everyone else.*

Evan: *You were brave. You helped people. You helped them get out.*

Me: *No. People died.*

Evan: *But some people lived. A lot of people lived. You lived.*

His words look so nice written there that I want to believe in them.

chapter fifteen

I'm a little groggy today because I stayed up way too late texting Evan last night. I even went back to sleep for two hours after my mom and Ben left. But now it's the afternoon and I have my Thursday session with Brenda. I drag two beach chairs out of the storage closet in the hallway of our apartment and set them up outside in front of the welcome mat. I sit down to wait. In my jeans. I wear them now instead of pajamas. Because it makes my mom happy. And Brenda. And me.

If I poke my toes through the slats of the railing, the sun hits them just right.

When Brenda arrives, she stops in the courtyard to look up at me.

"You're outside already."

I nod. "Hurry up before I chicken out."

She scurries up the stairs and sits down next to me. She has her burgundy dreads piled on top of her head and she's wearing a short skirt. It's kind of awkward for her to sit in a low beach chair dressed that way, but she doesn't complain about it. She simply kicks off her boots and sticks her toes through the slats of the railing like me.

"It's wonderful to see you out here. How have you been?" she asks.

"Good. Ben's going to be in a play."

"That's exciting."

I pick at the edge of the plastic armrest on my beach chair. "He wants me to go. He wants me to be there."

"I see." Brenda scribbles something down. "When is it?"

"June. Right before school gets out."

"And you have concerns?"

"Of course I have concerns. I don't leave my apartment. How am I supposed to go to my brother's play?"

"Do you want to go?"

"Yes."

"Then we'll make sure you do." She wiggles her toes, trying to stretch them out farther into the sun. "We have about seven weeks to work on this." She looks at me for confirmation that I'm on board. I nod. "Great. We'll make it a goal then. We can even practice with some visualization."

"What's that?"

"Visualization can trick your brain into thinking something has already happened. Like it exists as a memory."

"That makes sense, I guess."

I say that even though I'm not sure I actually mean it. It just seems like my brain would know whether I've actually been to my brother's play or not.

Brenda keeps wiggling her toes and adjusts her skirt so it doesn't ride up. These chairs really aren't made for an outfit like hers, but I try not to think about it because I don't want to move or go back inside. This surprises me. I'm relieved to feel this comfortable out here.

"So. What else have you been up to?" she asks.

"I've actually been doing a lot of writing."

"Good. That's great, really." She puts that down in her notebook and looks back at me. "What have you been writing, exactly?"

"A bunch of stuff." The turquoise water of the pool glistens below us, and I can almost trick myself into thinking I'm about to dive right in. "And I wrote another letter."

"Fantastic. I encourage that." She smiles. Proud. "Do you think I could see what you wrote?"

I shift uncomfortably.

"What's wrong?" she asks me.

"Well, I wrote a letter." I gnaw at the corner of my thumbnail. "But I delivered it. Or technically, Ben delivered it. I didn't know I was supposed to show it to you first."

She jots something else down. "It's okay, Morgan. Maybe I didn't give you the best direction on that. How did it go?"

"It went really well, actually. I wrote it to Evan."

"The new boy? Your neighbor?" She gestures to the shredded screen door of Evan's apartment.

"Yep."

"Can I ask you what you wrote?"

I pick at the shredded knee of my jeans. "I basically told him the truth about me."

"Which is what?"

"You know."

"But I'd like to hear it in your words." She has her pen poised, ready to write it down.

"I said I've been scared to leave my apartment since October fifteenth, but that he reminds me of the things I'm missing. He didn't seem freaked out."

"I'm glad to hear that."

"We hung out. We're friends. I need a friend."

"What about your other friends? From before. Do you miss them?"

"Of course. But it's nice having a new friend."

"Mm-hm. New friends are nice. But old friends are nice, too. Don't you think?"

"I wouldn't know. I don't talk to them."

"That was your decision, not theirs."

"Thanks for reminding me."

We look out at the pool. The surface of it twinkles against the sun. I wish Brenda would understand why new friends might be easier for me than old friends. And that I might like Evan as more than a friend. She must sense that.

"If I'm not supposed to send letters, why did you want me to go to the mailbox before?"

"Oh, we would've mailed your letter." She taps her pen against her notebook. "But we would've talked about it first. About what you'd written. We didn't get that far. I'm sorry. If it makes you feel better, I think you did the right thing giving your letter to Evan. It sounds like he responded well. It's a positive step for you. I'm glad you did it."

She sounds pretty confident. Of course, she always sounds confident. But she sounds so confident about this particular thing that it does make me feel better.

We talk some more. She asks me all the regular things that she always asks: How am I sleeping? How am I eating? Have I needed any emergency pills? And then we talk about new things. Like Evan. And why I wanted to let him in. Every week she tries to chip away at something else. Like she's an archaeologist and I'm the ancient skeleton she's discovered buried underneath a bunch of dirt somewhere far away.

When our hour is up, she tells me I should keep writing letters. "But maybe I could read them. If you're okay with that."

I nod because I trust Brenda. I mean, I mostly trust Brenda. Because if I trusted her completely, I'd probably tell her everything.

"What do you say we work up to trying the stairs? Just a little farther. Maybe a little on Tuesday and more on Thursday?"

I look at the steps in front of me.

They lead down to the courtyard.

The pool.

The mailboxes.

The front gate.

The world.

The top step seems close enough, but the bottom one looks like it's a mile away. I want to say no, but then I think of everything that's outside that gate. There are bad things, but there are good things, too. I have to keep moving forward if I'm going to stand a chance at finding them again.

"Okay. I'll try," I say.

chapter sixteen

My mom's cell phone rings after dinner, and she excuses herself to go outside and sit on the stairs to talk. That's where she goes when she wants privacy since our apartment is about the size of a shoe box. I have an idea of who it might be.

Someone related to my dad.

Someone with the same olive skin and big dark eyes.

Someone who wants answers.

Someone who is sad.

Someone who is sick with worry, but also frustrated.

Someone who has talked to him.

Someone who knows where he is.

Ben is buzzing around. Literally buzzing. Like a bee.

"Buzz," he goes. "Buzz, buzz, buzz." He flies around the apartment, chasing me from the kitchen to the living room to the hallway to our room. "I'm gonna sting you! You better watch out!"

I run in front of him, swooping around him when it seems he's finally gotten close enough to actually get me. "I'm too quick for you," I say as I dash back down the hall, past the school portraits that hang there. The frames are shaped like school buses. Each window on the bus is for a different year, from kindergarten through twelfth grade. My eleventh and twelfth grade windows are empty. And a shinier, more optimistic version of me occupies all the other years.

Ben is laughing so hard that he can't run straight. He goes *thump thump* into the walls of the hall.

"Be careful," I call. "Don't knock down the pictures."

I finally let him catch me on the couch. He takes his finger and pokes me. "Ha! Got you! Zap!"

I pull my hand to my shoulder where he stung me. "Ow! That hurts!"

He laughs. "Buzz, buzz."

"You're too cute to sting people." I pull him onto my lap and smother him with kisses. He tries to keep buzzing, but he's practically choking on laughter. "Calm down, little bee," I say.

Ben finally catches his breath, settles down, and glazes over at a cartoon on television. I realize my mom has been gone a long time. I untangle Ben from my lap and sit him down on the other side of the couch so I can get up to check on her.

I step out on the welcome mat. It's amazing how easy it is to stand here now that I've done it a few times. And it feels good to do it, too. I see my mom sitting on the bottom step. She's still wearing her hospital scrubs. Her phone call is done. But I hardly notice that because I can really only focus on the fact that Evan is towering in front of her. He's got his wet suit slung over one shoulder and his surfboard under his arm. The look on his face is very serious. He's listening to my mom. She is staring up at him and saying things. I want to see her face. She's telling him something important. I know this because of the way Evan watches her.

And then I hear her say, "She's working through some problems. It could take a while."

And right then, Evan's eyes shoot up and meet mine. We lock on to each other for a split second until my mom turns her head to look at me, too.

chapter seventeen

I run to my room.

I slam the door.

I fall onto my stomach on top of my bed.

I bury my face in my pillow.

I sob.

Ben calls my name.

I can hear his feet racing down the hall toward our room.

My mom intercepts him.

She tells him everything is okay and to please go practice his spelling words.

A few seconds later, there's a knock outside my room. My mom doesn't wait for me to say come in or don't. She just opens the door and lets herself inside.

She sits on the edge of my bed.

She places her hand on my back.

She rubs tiny, soothing circles.

"What's wrong?" she asks.

Seriously? "You're kidding, right?" I mumble into my pillow. "I didn't think I had to worry about my mom convincing people not to hang out with me."

She pauses for a second like she's racking her brain. Like what she said didn't happen only one minute ago. "Do you mean Evan? Is that what you think I told him? Not to hang out with you?"

"Um, yes. I heard you. You told him I was all messed up and too much trouble."

"You know I didn't say that."

"I don't remember your exact words, but that was pretty much your message."

"Well, you didn't hear me then. You didn't hear me thank him." She knocks her hip into mine to get me to scoot over so she can lie down next to me. "He's good for you."

I roll onto my side to face her, rubbing the tears and snot off my face. "What?"

"You've changed. It started when Evan moved in."

"You really think so?"

"Yep. I've seen some of the old Morgan coming back."

And of course I want to believe her. But now I can only think the opposite.

"But maybe I *am* too much work. I mean, Evan's in high school. He should go be in high school. He doesn't need all this."

"Need all what?"

"This. Me. Come on, you don't think my life is just a little bit messy?"

"I think you're a girl who went through a horrible thing, something no mom ever wants to think about their kid going through. But I also think you're smart and capable. I think you're working hard to get better. I think you want to get better. I think you *will* get better."

"When?"

"When you're ready. I believe in you." She runs her hand over the top of my head. She smooths the strands back that are stuck to my tears. "I saw you outside. You were on the welcome mat."

"Uh-huh."

"Do you do that now?"

"Sometimes. Brenda wanted to try it."

"But you did it. And you feel okay about it?"

"Yeah. I mean, it's not very far."

"But it's outside. It's something."

"Yeah."

"Well, don't stop."

"I won't."

"Good."

We lie on the bed there. My mom strokes my hair, and I listen to her breathe. She takes in slow, deep breaths. She seems exhausted. Like she could fall asleep right here.

"Who was on the phone?" I ask to keep her from drifting off. It's too early to fall asleep.

"Your grandma," she murmurs. "With an update."

"Did she see Dad?"

"Something like that. They know where he is. For now."

"Where?"

"San Diego. As we suspected."

"Is he okay?"

My mom closes her eyes. Sighs. "He's the same."

I think of what that means. Of what my dad has become. He used to be dependable. He used to tell the best jokes and carve the best jack-o'-lanterns. He used to come to my swim meets and keep track of my split times in a tiny notebook he kept in his back pocket.

He used to love me.

I used to *know* he loved me.

But now, I don't trust him. And I don't want him in my life until he gives me a reason to find that trust again. But that doesn't stop me from missing him. It only makes it worse.

chapter eighteen

A week passes, and on the last Thursday of April, after my mom and Ben leave for the day, the rain comes down like a last hurrah to April Showers. It pounds against the roof all morning. It slides down the windows and onto the ground. It glides down the front door and soaks the welcome mat. It smacks the surface of the swimming pool, making the water bounce up into the air.

Bam, bam, bam it goes.

I turn the TV up loud so I won't hear it.

I don't like the rain.

I don't like the rain anymore.

I used to love it. I would walk in it. I would swim in it. I would spin around in it. I would let the cold of it spatter against my face and my eyelashes.

When I was five, I had pink-and-purple rain boots with cat ears and whiskers on them. I had a jacket to match. I had knobby knees covered in Hello Kitty Band-Aids. And hair that hung in fishtail braids. One Saturday afternoon, the rain pounded on the roof and slid down the windowpanes. My dad put on a raincoat, then helped me pull on my cat boots. He handed me an umbrella, took my hand, and led me out the door, giddy and grinning.

"Let's go find some puddles," he said. I knew I was in for a good time.

We walked around the neighborhood, splashing through the water. I jumped from a curb to make the biggest splat I could. He clapped for me when I leapt off a picnic table in the park and landed in a muddy puddle that bounced up and left dirty remnants on my sweatpants and his jacket. He showed me how to make bigger splashes by hitting the heel of my boot just right. We laughed and splashed and held hands through the puddles in the park as my braids dripped over my shoulders. We walked down the street, past the cars driving by with their headlights on in the middle of the day.

Whoosh, whoosh, whoosh.

Whip, whip, whip.

"Fun can be free," my dad told me, squeezing my soggy hand. "And water is water no matter where you find it."

When we came home, drenched and laughing, my mom stuck me right into a warm bath while my dad made hot chocolate with more mini marshmallows than my mom would ever allow in one sitting. Once I was dry and bundled up, my dad and I sat on the couch, listened to the rain, and drank hot chocolate in our slippers. My legs weren't even long enough for my toes to hit the floor.

"I love the rain," I announced, swinging my feet back and forth.

"Me too," he said through a sip of hot chocolate, his words echoing in the almost empty mug. "We are people who love the rain."

It was official. That would be our thing. We would be rain people. My dad and I.

But now I hate the rain.

Because it is too loud with memories of October fifteenth.

Which is why I pace the floors of my apartment today.

I wonder if I need an emergency pill.

I stand in front of my list.

I do the things it says.

I breathe.

I think of good things.

I tell myself I'm okay. *You are not dying.*

I count down the minutes until Brenda gets here.

By the time Brenda knocks on the door, the rain has stopped. I open up right away. She stands on my welcome mat in rubber motorcycle boots and a matching biker jacket. Only she would have rain gear like that. Outside, the ground is still damp. There are a few puddles in the courtyard. But the sun is out and it's trying really hard to make things bright and cheerful.

Brenda steps back from the door. She gestures to the stairs. "Shall we?"

She takes the first step. I know I have to go farther than before. I made it to the top of the stairs on Tuesday. I nod my head. I take a step.

The first step down feels like I'm jumping out of an airplane. It's a descent that makes my heart pound. I want my parachute to open with that jerky motion that'll pull me back up for a second. Only a tiny tug and I could be by my front door again.

Brenda's boots smack the fourth step and then the fifth one.

She doesn't turn around. She just expects me to be right behind her.

She has faith in me.

I try really hard, but I only make it a few more steps. Everything is spinning. My toes tingle. My fingertips prickle. I have to hold on to the railing to steady myself. I grip it, actually. I grip it so tightly that my fingernails dig into the rotting wood of its underside.

I make it halfway down.

I stop.

I sit.

Brenda turns to me and I shake my head. That's it. That's all I can do. She walks back up a few steps and settles down next to me. She pats my knee. She's letting me know I did okay.

The stairs are still damp, and the wetness slowly seeps into the back of my jeans. I don't care. It reminds me I'm outside. It reminds me I did this.

"It was raining the day that everything happened." I start talking because I want to say something even though Brenda didn't ask me to.

"You've mentioned that before. Does it bother you?"

"Maybe things would've been different if it hadn't been raining."

"Why is that?"

"I don't know. It's just a feeling I have." That's half the story. It's the part that's a lie. I shake my head to clear it. "It's silly."

"Nothing is silly if you think it matters."

I nod my head, but I know I won't tell her anything more than that today. I started. But I had to stop.

We sit on the stairs.

We do the visualization stuff we talked about. In my mind, I've watched Ben's entire play, given a standing ovation, and returned home again. In reality, I'm still sitting on the stairs in front of my apartment.

When we're done pretending I've gone to Ben's play, we talk about letters and to whom I could write them.

"How about your dad?" Brenda asks.

I think of my grandma calling my mom last night and how tired it made her. "What's the point?"

"As I've told you before, it might be a useful exercise."

"I'd rather not try it."

She nods. "I understand how you might feel that way. But you should."

"Why? What makes you such an expert?"

She looks at me. I look at her. Her mouth quirks. She holds her hand out to shake my hand.

"I'm Dr. Brenda Gwynn. Have we met?"

"Sorry," I mumble. "I forgot you were an expert."

"It's okay." She tosses her dreadlocks over her shoulder and they thump against her back. "And I might be an expert in more ways than you realize when it comes to this particular thing, so will you listen to what I have to say?"

"Fine."

"I think it would be good for you to write a letter to your dad because there is something freeing about getting the words out. It's helpful to put the hurt and frustration onto the page. When you write it, you can think, *I'm letting this go.*"

I listen to her, but I don't look at her.

"It helped when you wrote the letter to Evan, right?"

"Yeah, but I'm not mad at Evan."

She nods. "I hear you. But anger is a horrible thing to cart around. Let's see if we can do something to help you with that."

"Okay."

The clouds move across the sky, leaving behind streaks of blue. The barely damp edges of pavement around a rain puddle have dried up under the sun since we've been here.

I thank her.

I go inside.

chapter nineteen

After I say goodbye to Brenda, I sit down at the computer to work. I finish up a paper that's due next week, and then our home phone rings. I answer. It's someone from a mental health facility in San Diego. They ask for my mom. They say they're calling regarding a Mr. Richard Grant. I know what this person would tell my mom if she were here.

They would say Richard Grant was found drunk.

They would say he was disorderly.

They would say he was deemed a danger to himself.

They would say he is on a seventy-two-hour involuntary psychiatric hold.

This is not the first time my mom has been my dad's emergency contact.

They can't tell me these things even though I could recite the details from memory.

They can't tell me because I'm a minor.

The woman on the phone is kind and has a Southern drawl. The words ooze out of her mouth. "Please have your mama call us," she tells me.

I scribble down a number my mom can call when she gets home from work and is tired and dirty and has a headache. I refuse to bother her with it right now. If it were the first time, like a year and a half ago, then maybe. But it's not. I won't interrupt her during her shift. I thank the lady on the phone.

"You take care now," she says before we disconnect.

I slip to the floor and don't move. I don't do anything. I can't. I stay still to try to keep my heart from beating out of my chest like I'm in a movie about some freaky zombie invasion.

The thing is, I sometimes have to remind myself that my dad was good once. He was fun. And inspiring. He took me to play in the rain. He taught me things. He was a dad.

Ben was three months old the first time my dad met him. My brother, my mom, and I stood among hundreds of others on the blazing hot asphalt of the parking lot of the Army base, waiting for the buses to roll up with all the soldiers returning from deployment. We were lost in a sea of red, white, and blue pompoms and miniature American flags. I held up a homemade WELCOME HOME sign. I'd made it the night before using glitter glue and rainbow markers. I was eleven.

The buses finally rolled up, and the soldiers exited in camouflage uniforms and scanned the crowd. They looked for their families. They looked for the ones they loved. I waved. I jumped up and down. I couldn't spot my dad in all the people who looked the same. I wanted to find him. Desperately. Somehow I thought spotting him instantly would prove I hadn't forgotten him. Because sometimes I was afraid I had. Like weeks before when my sixth grade science teacher had told us how people either had attached or unattached earlobes. I felt mine. They were unattached and had tiny ladybug stud earrings in them. I knew my mom's earlobes were unattached like mine. So were Ben's. But I had to dig up a picture of my dad from our computer when I got home from school in order to see what his earlobes did. They were attached. I hadn't remembered.

But that day in the parking lot, I knew my dad when he started running toward us. He pulled me into a tight bear hug that made me safe and whole again. My mom cried happy tears and put Ben in his arms. My dad looked down at him in awe. Amazed. Our family was on the local news that night because reporters always like to find the soldier returning from deployment who is meeting their baby for the first time. It tugs at heartstrings. It makes people cry. It drives home the fact that military families make huge sacrifices. We were that family that day. My dad was that soldier. Ben was that baby.

When we got home, everyone was hungry for lunch, but my mom had to nurse Ben and put him down for a nap. So my dad told me with a wink and a squeeze of my shoulder that it was about time he taught his favorite girl how to make grilled cheese sandwiches. And tomato soup. It had always been his first-choice meal. It had always been *our* meal. He called it comfort food. He said it was the thing he craved when he was sitting in the desert eating an MRE in the dusty dirt. He got the soup started and lined everything else up on the counter. Bread. Butter. Cheese. Piping hot griddle. He made the first one and we shared it right there in the kitchen, laughing as we wrapped the oozing cheese around our fingertips and sucked it into our mouths. He helped me make three more sandwiches and manage the soup after that. And when everything was done, the three of us sat down to eat. We were together again. Things were as they should be.

It was good until it wasn't.

Over the next four years, my dad was deployed again. Eight months, then twelve. He'd enlisted when I was in preschool. As a twenty-three-year-old father, who'd kicked around for four years trying to provide for his family, I imagine the Army seemed like an honorable way to do what was best for us. But the after-effects of 9/11 lasted longer than anyone had anticipated, and every time my dad thought he'd finally have extended time back with us, he was redeployed sooner rather than later. It took its toll. He returned from the last tour angrier and more distant. He drank too much. More than I'd ever seen. He didn't spend time at home. He stopped hugging me and coming to my swim meets. We didn't make grilled cheese sandwiches. He fought with my mom in hushed tones that grew louder through the walls. When he was around, he paid more attention to Ben than to me. I decided this was because Ben was only four and too little to know a better version of our dad existed. I think my dad liked that. I was fifteen. He knew the only thing he could give me was disappointment.

My dad still isn't the same. And neither am I. He is in a psychiatric lockdown facility against his own will. I stay locked up in an apartment.

I have pathetic DNA.

So when Evan knocks on my door a little after four p.m.—I

know it's him because he calls my name through the wood—I can't let him in.

He keeps knocking.

He calls my name once more.

I sit perfectly still.

I stay that way until he leaves.

chapter twenty

Evan knocks at the door every fifteen minutes. He calls my name and jiggles the metal knob. He texts me messages I don't read. I've turned the sound off on my phone, but I can hear the vibration against the countertop as his texts come through. When the evening comes, he's outside my door again. He sounds panicked by now. I haven't turned any lights on. I haven't turned on the TV. The curtains are closed. I haven't made a single sound. I've just lain still on the floor in the living room for two hours. Shadows slip silently, hitting my feet and then my ankles. Next my calves and my knees. My stomach. My chest. My eyes.

I can hear Evan outside when my mom and Ben come home just after six p.m. He calls to my mom and she comes bounding up the stairs. I can hear the *boom boom* of her feet skipping steps. I can hear her keys in the lock. She bursts through the door and drops the mail in front of her feet. She looks everywhere and finally at the floor.

She finds me.

She rushes over.

She hovers above me, squinting.

She whispers my name.

She kneels down at my side.

I don't have words for her. I don't have explanations. But when she puts her hands on my cheeks, I know she thinks I might be dead. She lifts me up into her arms, holding me to her chest when she sees I'm still as here as I can be.

Ben is watching us. He's fidgeting. I can tell he's scared. I feel guilty for letting him see me this way.

"Evan," my mom says gently, "can you take Ben next door for a little bit?"

Evan doesn't move at first. He only stares down at me, and I know he's trying to figure out what he thinks about this other side of me. And that makes me wish I'd never told him anything. I wish I'd never opened the door and let him in. Because what I can see right now is the thing I never wanted: he pities me.

"Evan, please," my mom says.

"Yeah, sure. Right. Come on, buddy." Evan nudges Ben's shoulder and pulls him through the front door.

"What happened?" my mom asks me, reaching over to turn on the light.

I lie down again, flat against the floor. I run my hands across the carpet. I tell her about the phone call. I tell her where my dad is. I tell her what I realized.

"I'm going to be exactly like him."

"No. You're not." She says the words like they're nonnegotiable, like brushing my teeth or eating leafy green vegetables. "That's why we have Brenda. I won't let that happen to you."

"But I'm trying. I'm trying so hard. And I can barely get out the front door."

"Don't you see? You've taken the first step forward. Your dad is only taking steps backward. Everyone, all of us, we want to help him. He doesn't want it. You can't help someone who doesn't want help. I tried to tell that to your grandma when she called the other night. She's just a mom who wants her son to be okay. I get it. But he doesn't want help." My mom pushes my hair off my face. "You want help, right? You want to get better." She asks me like she needs me to say it. Like she needs me to confirm it for her own peace of mind.

"Yeah," I say.

And I do want to get better. I want it in a way that makes it feel like a necessity. I just don't know how to get there. What I'm doing doesn't seem like enough.

Later that night, my mom plunks Ben into the bath and scrubs his head clean with his apple-scented shampoo.

I hear him through the wall.

"Morgan's gonna come to my play, right, Mom? She's coming, right?"

I can tell my mom is scooping water into a big cup and pouring it over Ben's head because I can hear him sputtering against the bubbles. He does that when they run down his face, too close to his mouth.

"She'll try her best, Benjamin."

"She better come."

I sink into my pillow and scrub my fists against my eyelids. I try to picture myself at Ben's play in six weeks. I want to go, but the idea seems absurd. It really does. He can never know that.

"Why was Morgan on the floor?" Ben asks.

"She had a long day."

"I think she was tired."

"Yeah, she probably was."

"She should've gone to bed."

"Yeah."

"Do you think she's sick?"

"She's fine. She'll be fine."

The screen on my cell phone lights up after Ben is asleep and our room is dark.

Evan: *What's going on? Talk to me.*

Me: *Not now.*

Evan: *Seriously? What the hell, Morgan?*

His annoyance shouts at me in the dark.

I delete his message.

I shut off the phone.

I shove it into the drawer of my nightstand.

I slam the drawer shut.

I roll over to face the wall.

I try to sleep.

I can't.

Why does everyone always want to talk?

The day that everything happened, I had to talk to so many people. I had to talk to police officers and counselors. At first, we all ended up on the soggy grass of the football field. It was the emergency evacuation center for my school. So many of us were saturated from the pounding rain. Tents were haphazardly erected and umbrellas were handed out. Students huddled in clumps under tents or stood three to an umbrella. Obviously nobody expected a downpour when they thought up my school's evacuation plan. Everything on the field was chaotic. Tears. Primal screams when bad news came. We all wanted to leave, but it was where we had to wait until we could be released to our parents. They had to check us off on a list. We had to be accounted for.

I borrowed a phone to call my mom and tell her I was okay. She was so relieved to hear my voice. She was standing across the street from my school with a bunch of other parents who were waiting for news. As soon as she heard about students arriving at the emergency room of the hospital where she worked, she'd raced to my school to find me.

At the field, we had to say where we'd been when everything happened. When I said I'd been in English class, I was put into a separate line. The language arts building line. We were the ones who had really seen things. They were going to question us one by one.

It was in this line that I finally found Sage. We crashed into each other and sobbed. She'd talked to Brianna and Chelsea. They'd gotten out okay. I was so glad to hear that, because I hadn't been able to get ahold of them. So many people left their backpacks when they ran. So many people didn't have their phones.

After I talked to a police officer on the field and he found out what I saw and where I hid, he wanted me to go to the police station. They needed to talk to me more in depth. It was getting late, so my mom arranged for Ben to go home with a friend from his after-school program so she could drive me downtown.

Once there, I sat at a table in an office and stared at a poster of the schedule for my school's football team. It was orange and blue and had a picture of Neptune crashing through sea foam. He gripped a trident and stared back at me. We still had four games left in the season.

My mom sat at my side, pushing tissues into my fist and rubbing her knuckles in tiny circles across my back. I was finally dry. But the rain had made the blood spread out on my shirt, resulting in the most morbid-looking tie-dye job ever.

A pretty blond woman, who was tall like a professional basketball player, sat across from me, writing stuff down on a notepad. Kind of like Brenda, but not all the way like Brenda. A digital recorder was set up, too.

I had to give statements.

I had to say where I was sitting.

I had to say where I ran.

I had to say where I hid.

I had to say what I saw.

I didn't tell them everything.

She wrote my words down and said thank you.

A counselor visited me last. He told me what I was feeling was normal. He said it was okay to feel angry or sad or any of the emotions I had and that right now I might not feel anything at all. He gave me a card with a phone number on it. He said I could call it twenty-four hours a day, seven days a week. He said someone would always be there to talk to me no matter what. He said I should go home and eat. Then sleep. He said he'd check in with me in a few days. He did. I told him I was fine. It was a lie.

My mom and I picked up Ben on the way home. It was after eight p.m. He'd been asleep already and he stayed that way in the car. I was glad, because I think my appearance would've scared him. We would tell him the next morning when my shirt was in the washing machine and my hair was brushed. But that night, my mom carried him to the apartment and put him to bed with his clothes on.

I had a bowl of cereal for dinner. It was hard to keep it down.

I stayed in my mom's bed that night. I curled into her side. Her flannel nightgown was soft against my face. She cradled me against her like I was small. It felt safe and warm. It was the only way I could sleep.

chapter twenty-one

All weekend, my mom fields phone calls from my grandma about my dad. She wants to know what to do and whom to call and where to be. She wants to know how we can make sure this time is different.

My mom tells her she shouldn't bother getting her hopes up. My mom says she's tried a million times. She says she has washed her hands of it. She doesn't have time for this. She has bigger problems now. I know that bigger problem is me.

And right now, she is worried about me.

I know this because of the way she watches me move through the apartment. She looks up from the stuff she's stirring in a saucepan to observe me. On Saturday night, she stops reading to Ben midsentence and eyes me as I cross in front of his bed to pull clean pajamas out of my dresser. I haven't combed my hair since Thursday morning. It's long and tangled. She wonders, out loud to Ben, why I'm so quiet. She wants to know if I've eaten. Or done my homework. Or brushed my teeth.

She is afraid I've taken a step back.

She wants Brenda to come.

She wants Brenda to help.

On Sunday, she finally convinces me I need to make an emergency call to Brenda. She picks up right away. I tell her about my dad.

"I'm so sorry, Morgan." Brenda's voice is comforting, like an oversize sweatshirt. There's a part of me that wishes she were here. I want to sit on the steps with her just long enough to feel the sun on my face. And then I'd go inside and shut the door again.

On the phone, Brenda asks me how I feel. She says I'm talking slower and quieter than I usually do. She wants to know if I notice. I tell her I don't feel electric. I'm sapped of energy. I'm used to feeling like I can't stop fidgeting. But this thing with my dad has just made me numb. All I want to do is curl up in pajamas and stare at the wall. It's different from the way I feel when I need to take my emergency pill.

"Do you want to hurt yourself?" She clears her throat. "I'm sorry I have to ask that, but it's important for you to tell me if you're having those kinds of thoughts."

I tell her no. And that's the truth. I couldn't do that to my mom. Or Ben. I feel tired and immobile, but I don't want to die. "I want to sleep."

We keep talking. I'm not even sure how to put the way I'm feeling into words.

"It's okay not to know," Brenda says. "Maybe you need to figure it out. And we can work on it some more on Tuesday. You can call me before then if you need to talk."

I thank her and hang up. Maybe I should've told her she might as well quit now, because I will probably end up just like my dad.

Evan stops by a few times over the weekend. He has probably texted, too. I haven't turned my phone back on to know for sure.

I haven't even taken it out of the drawer I shoved it in. I ask my mom and Ben to tell Evan to go away.

They don't say those exact words. They're nicer than that.

I don't go near the door when he comes. I stay on the couch. Or in my bed. Or I hover in the hallway. Ben tells him I'm sick. My mom says we're having some family issues we need to deal with.

"That boy is going to lose his patience with you," my mom says, shutting the door. "You should talk to him."

"I can't. Not yet."

I watch the surfing DVD Evan gave me. I watch it over and over again. I play it on the computer. I wear my headphones. I hear the wind and the laughter of his friends in my ears. I still envy the freedom of Evan sliding down that wave. I still wish I could stand in the sand there. I wish I could cheer. I wish I could be something other than what I am.

chapter twenty-two

Monday morning comes and my grandma calls. She is the only grandma I have ever known. She's my dad's mom. My mom's parents died before I was born. But I'd visit my dad's parents every July. Grandpa Ben—the grandpa who was so grand, my little brother was named after him—would take me to the county fair to buy me cotton candy as big as my head. When I was in middle school, he rode the flippiest, turniest, spinniest rides with me even though he was way older than anyone else going on them.

When I was sixteen and the ink was barely dry on my driver's license, my grandpa died suddenly of a heart attack. He'd been working on his beloved Bel Air when it happened. My grandma heard a crash. She ran to the garage and found him on the ground next to a pile of stuff that must have fallen from the tool shelf when he bumped into it as he fell.

People said the kinds of things people say to make everyone feel better when someone dies. They said, "At least he went doing something he loved."

Those words didn't make me feel better. I missed him when he was gone.

At the funeral, my grandma told me my grandpa had left his car to me. I felt so special. I assumed that because he adored that car, he must have adored me. To this day, I have no doubt this is true, but sometimes I wonder if that car was nothing but bad luck.

Last summer, I drove Ben down the coast to visit our grandma without my mom. I was hoping to take my brother on all the same rides at the fair. He wasn't tall enough. But I did get to buy him cotton candy as big as his head.

This morning, my grandma tells my mom everything that happened between yesterday morning and now. My mom stands in the bathroom getting ready for work. She has to set her cell phone on the back of the toilet and put it on speaker so she can use her hands to brush her teeth and comb her hair. I listen from the hallway, but my mom doesn't know. Ben can't hear because he's eating breakfast in the other room with the TV on. She thinks I'm with him. She wouldn't want us to hear this.

My grandma's brittle voice comes through the speaker. "When I went to pick him up, the people there said he has PTSD. They gave me some phone numbers. They said it would be a good idea to try to get him into a program, and that he needs to stop drinking, too. The drinking makes everything worse."

"No kidding," my mom says.

Anybody I've ever been related to knows this already. Even my grandma knows this. But she says it like yesterday was the first time she'd ever heard it.

My grandma tells my mom she thanked the doctors and walked out the door. She says my dad sat in the passenger seat and didn't say a word. At home, he sat on the couch and still didn't say anything. She said it was like he was a teenager. She chuckles. My mom doesn't. My grandma says she cooked all day. Eventually my dad migrated to the kitchen to watch. He sat in a chair and made promises that he would research the alcohol counseling programs listed in the pamphlets my grandma had fanned out in the middle of the table. And while he made those promises, she made him everything he always loved to eat. She mashed potatoes and drowned them in gravy. She served the potatoes with a pork roast she'd marinated for hours in the fridge. She made a three-layer chocolate cake with homemade buttercream frosting for dessert. When my dad ate all the food, it made my grandma think he was okay.

"He had his appetite." She says this as if it should've been proof that he was getting better.

My mom explains that what's wrong with my dad isn't like having the flu. Eating might not mean anything. It's something in his brain *and* his body. It's something different.

My grandma doesn't pay attention. Instead, she tells my mom that after dinner, my dad took a long, hot shower. She says she washed his clothes. She stuck her hands in the pockets of his pants, but didn't find anything aside from two dollars, some change, and a crumpled-up fortune from a fortune cookie. Later, when it was dark and everyone was tired, my uncle Matt came over with three pairs of jeans and five new T-shirts for my dad.

"He brought every color." My grandma says it like it matters. As if my dad wants to be the best-dressed homeless vet in San Diego.

My grandma says my dad folded the clothes neatly and piled them into a duffel bag. He put his new toothbrush and toothpaste in a side pocket. There was also soap. And deodorant. And two packages of brand-new underwear still wrapped in the plastic bag they came in. My grandma lists everything like she's reading off a checklist for sixth grade camp.

"It was like he was embarrassed to take everything. Like he wanted to shove it all in the duffel and not look at it."

I can picture her hovering in the doorway, watching him.

"Why are you packing?" she probably asked.

I can see her walking over and touching my dad on the shoulder. Her touch would've made him flinch. I've seen the way he flinches when people try to touch him, even if he loved them once. I knew to never sneak up on him to give him a hug. He became skittish even after only one tour in Afghanistan. I knew I had to make sure he saw me before I climbed into his lap and hung around his neck. And then he'd settle me into the crook of his arm and we'd watch TV together. He got worse with more tours. When I was older and he was sad all the time, I'd feel bad when I startled him as I came around the corner and into a room. I'd tell him I was sorry and try to hug him. He'd flinch at the contact and shrug his way out of my hug.

"I begged him to stay," my grandma says through the phone. "Stay as long as you need. We can get help. We can fix this." We've all said those things before. But as much as we say the words, my dad never hears them.

The last time my dad was home about a year and a half ago, my mom said the opposite. She told him he couldn't stay anymore. "You need to go," she said.

Ben and I had his railroad tracks set up in the living room. I

133

was trying to distract him while our mom and dad fought by the front door. They were only hissing at each other at first. But then my mom's voice got louder. Like she needed to be heard. It was early in the morning and my dad hadn't come home the night before. He'd been arrested and sat in a cell all night to get sober. It wasn't the first time. He didn't call my mom to let her know. He left her at home to worry.

"No more," my mom said that day.

My dad's key was still in the lock. She wouldn't let him inside the apartment. And after that day, he never came home again.

"Tell her what really happened," my uncle Matt yells through the speaker now. "Tell her how he drank every last drop of alcohol in this house and started yelling and screaming. Tell them how I wanted to call the police, but you wouldn't let me."

"Stop!" my grandma cries. "Just, please, stop."

But my uncle doesn't stop. "We told him he could stay if he went to rehab. He didn't like that ultimatum. He never does." I can picture him pacing across the bright yellow linoleum floor of my grandma's kitchen, running his hand through his thinning hair.

My grandma starts to cry.

Deep down inside, I'm sure she knew my dad would never agree to get help. But that didn't stop her from hoping this time would be different.

"I tried to stay up all night," she says. "But I got too tired. I fell asleep in front of the TV. He slipped out the front door. I woke up still holding the remote control." Her voice cracks. "He's gone."

"And so is most of her jewelry, by the way!" my uncle yells in the background.

"It's not your fault. He's sick. You have to stop blaming yourself," my mom says.

"Tell her, Carol! Tell her what a colossal waste of time this is." My uncle is so loud that my mom has to switch the speaker off.

She balances the phone between her ear and her shoulder. She mumbles something, then stops to listen. She knots her hair on top of her head. She runs a blush brush along her cheekbones. She speaks calmly to my grandma. She sounds like Brenda. She tells her she did her best.

"I'll call you tonight," my mom finally says. "I need to take Ben to school. I have to go to work."

My grandma must ask her something about me, because I hear my mom say, "She's still at home." She pauses to listen to whatever my grandma says back, but then my mom interrupts her. "We're working on it," she says. I can detect the clip in her voice. It's right below the surface. It's a tone full of frustration. I don't know if it's directed at my grandma or at me.

chapter twenty-three

I'm glad today is Tuesday. Brenda is coming. I haven't talked to her since my emergency call a couple days ago. I wait for her halfway down the stairs outside the front door of my apartment. She stops and stands still at the edge of the pool.

"Well, hi," she says. "Do you want to come over here?"

I shake my head no. She moves closer and asks if I want to go there. Still no. She moves closer again. It reminds me of when my mom and I would sit across from each other on the floor and reach our arms out to get Ben to walk back and forth between us. Only instead of gradually moving farther away, Brenda keeps closing the distance. Finally, she stands at the bottom of the stairs.

"How about here?"

I feel like this is her version of meeting in the middle. It's not the edge of the pool. It's not the center of the courtyard. It's only a few more steps from where I already am. I stand up. I grip the railing. I put one foot in front of me, and then the other. I take six steps until I'm standing at the bottom of the stairs.

Brenda takes my hand. She squeezes it. One squeeze. A squeeze that means everything without saying it.

"Sit," she says.

I do.

Brenda adjusts herself on the bottom step. She straightens her legs out in front of her, then crosses one purple-Chuck-Taylored foot over the other one. "Tell me about the rest of your weekend. How's your dad?"

"Not good."

"Mm-hm."

She doesn't seem surprised. And she shouldn't be. It's not like someone who gets hauled away on an involuntary psychiatric hold is expected to be in excellent condition after it happens. She asks me for more details, so I tell her what my grandma said.

"I see." She scribbles a note down. Her forehead wrinkles. I bet she doesn't want me to notice that. "I understand how that would be upsetting."

"It's just the same old thing. He only cares about himself."

"Oh, Morgan. I'm so sorry. I know it can seem like he's being selfish, but there's more to it than that. Are you feeling frustrated?"

"I'm not frustrated. That's not what's wrong with me."

She wrinkles her forehead again. "Then what is it?"

I know I have to tell her everything I haven't said out loud all weekend. I have to say the things I had on the tip of my tongue, but shoved back down my throat. I have to tell her all the things I've only thought. But it's hard to get the words out.

"It's just . . . How can you tell me, like, how do you *really* know, that I'm not going to be like him? It could happen, right? Fifty percent of me came from him."

Brenda looks at me. She looks at me hard and she looks at me long. "You are not like him."

"Yeah, right." I lean forward, elbows on my knees, and stare at the door of the apartment in front of me. There's a sign hanging on it that says LIFE IS BETTER AT THE BEACH.

Brenda taps me on the chin so I'll look at her. She holds her hand to her chest. She presses it firmly to her heart. "Your heart needs comfort and reassurance. Give it that. Don't be a victim. Be a survivor."

I shake my head. I try to undo the bad thoughts in there. I want to jiggle them loose and leave them on the ground in front of me. I don't want to be a victim.

"Look behind you," Brenda says. "Look how far you've come."

I'm afraid to turn around. I'm afraid it will look so far away that I'll want to run back inside and slam the door. But I do what Brenda says. I turn around. I look up the stairs. They are steep and there are a whole bunch of them. My front door is standing wide open. The Santa Ana winds blow in. I can picture the kitchen curtains with the light blue sailboats on them floating up into the air. The other thing I see is that it is a long way back up there. For me, at least. For someone who's been holed up in an apartment at Paradise Manor for the last six months, sitting here at the bottom of these stairs is a pretty big deal.

"Are you proud of yourself?" Brenda asks.

"I guess."

"I want you to own it, Morgan. Are you proud of yourself?"

"Yes."

"Good. You should be." She writes a note down. I picture it on the page. *Morgan is proud of herself.*

"I might've made a mistake, though."

"What do you mean?"

"I might've pushed Evan away."

"Why?"

I gnaw on the corner of my thumbnail. "I was trying to keep him out of the drama."

"Let's not call it drama, okay?"

"Okay. What should we call it then?"

"Oh, we could call it lots of things. But drama isn't one of them." Brenda crosses her feet in the other direction. "What is it that you're afraid Evan will do?"

Seriously? "Well, he could decide I'm crazy and never talk to me again."

"Does Evan strike you as someone who would do that?"

"Well, no. Not really."

"Do you like it when people tell you what to do and make decisions for you?"

"Of course not."

"Then why do you think it's okay for you to do that to Evan?"

Why does Brenda always have to be so smart?

"I think if Evan decides being friends with you is more than he can handle, he can make the choice for himself," Brenda says. "But it's not really fair that you make the choice for him. Unless you feel this relationship is potentially bad for you. Do you think that?"

"No. My mom even said she saw part of the old me coming back."

"Exactly." She writes down a note. Like she's really getting to the meat of things. "Be honest with Evan. Tell him what's bothering you. Then let him decide. My feeling is he'll say he's okay having a friend who's going through some stuff. And you'll feel better knowing he's okay with it."

chapter twenty-four

I decide to wait for Evan at the bottom of the stairs after Brenda leaves. I'm afraid I'll chicken out if I don't wait outside for him. Hopefully he'll come straight home from school so I don't have to sit out here forever. Because the stairs get more uncomfortable the longer I sit on them. I shift from butt cheek to butt cheek every few minutes as an hour passes by. I look at the water in the swimming pool and remember what it feels like to jump into it. I never hesitated to jump into the pool on hot days. It was the only good thing about Paradise Manor. After I scooped all the leaves out, I loved to leap in, swim to the bottom, and pop back through to the surface. It was one of the best feelings in the whole world.

And it hits me that I actually miss it.

I miss swimming.

At exactly that moment, Evan comes through the front gate. My heart rate speeds up and my palms get sweaty because I'm going to apologize. But then my heart sinks. Because Evan's not alone. He has Taylor Schneider with him. She only lives a few blocks from here, so it makes sense that they go to the same school now. And have probably fallen madly in love with each other.

She's blond.

She's cool.

She has a scar across her right shoulder where a bullet grazed her.

I know her, but we aren't friends. I don't dislike her or anything. We've just never hung out aside from swim team. We had matching team suits and the same lane assignment, but I wasn't friends with her like I was with Chelsea, Brianna, and Sage. Taylor was another long-distance swimmer on the team. But I held the school record and she didn't. And here she is now. She's standing in front of my feet. With Evan. And she's staring at me. They both are.

Everything about the way Evan is staring says he's annoyed with me. The muscle in his jaw is ticking, and he's gripping the strap of his backpack so tightly that his fingers have gone white. I want to talk, but there's no way I'm getting into it with Taylor here.

"Morgan, oh, my god!" Taylor gasps. "You're so . . . different." She grabs some chunks of her hair, pulls them up and lets them drop back down over her shoulders. I know what she's trying to say. She's trying to say my hair isn't streaked blond and shiny from chlorine anymore. I don't have a tan. Or muscle tone. I shrug my shoulders because there's nothing else I can really say. She's right.

But she's not exactly the same, either. The Taylor I remember was flirty and flouncy. She wore pink tutus and body glitter to football games. This new version of Taylor is ripped. The muscles in her arms are a billion times bigger and more defined. They aren't the kind of muscles you get from only swimming. They're the kind of muscles you get from lifting weights. At a gym that plays loud metal music. And is full of guys in tank tops with the sides cut out from top to bottom so you can see their stomach muscles through the gaps.

This Taylor is different. I don't know her.

"Thanks for ignoring me all weekend," Evan says, shaking me from my Taylor trance. His tone isn't kind, and I jerk back when his words feel like they've slapped me in the face.

"Sorry," I mumble.

"Well, at least you're outside," he says.

Taylor leans down and punches me playfully in the arm. "Oh, I knew it! I knew all that junk about you staying inside all the time was BS. I bet you sit out here every day, soaking up the rays, while we're all stuck in some boring classroom. You've got it all figured out."

I know she can tell by looking at me that what she said isn't true. I wish I could tell her that it is. I wish I were capable of fooling the system like that. But Evan and I know the truth. We both know that my being all the way down here on the bottom step, practically in the courtyard, is not even close to typical.

Taylor grabs on to the stair railing and tries to maneuver her way around me. That's when I realize I'm blocking the two of them from getting to Evan's apartment. They want to go inside together, and I'm in the way. I scramble up and dust off the back of my jeans.

"Sorry, geez. I'll move."

"Evan's teaching me to surf," Taylor says brightly. She's

wearing a tight black tank top with the mascot of her new school on it. A snarling wolverine. And I can see the keloid scar from the bullet on her muscular shoulder. It's thick and shiny and red.

"Oh, wow." I look at Evan, and he shrugs. "That's really cool of you."

And of course Evan should teach Taylor to surf. Taylor is what Evan deserves. She's a pretty girl who has a zest for life and wants to be with him in the ocean. And she knows how to flirt and be pretty. She used to wear a bikini to practice instead of the dorky one-piece Speedo I wore simply because I associated it with bringing me good luck. We shared a lane with the league-winning foursome of senior guys who consistently won the 4x100 free-style race, and in between sets, Taylor would hoist herself halfway out of the pool to grab her water bottle from the pool deck. All the guys in our lane would watch her, checking out her butt while she drank. She'd tell them to stop looking, playfully kicking water at their faces. Maybe she'll do that to Evan today. Out in the ocean.

She skitters up the stairs, but Evan stays behind, leaning into me. "Why did you blow me off?"

"I was a mess. I needed some space."

"Well, you made that clear."

I can't believe how differently this conversation is going from the way I'd hoped. "I didn't want you to see me like that." I say this under my breath, through gritted teeth, because Taylor is watching us.

Evan backs up. "No problem. I can take a hint."

"Evan, that's not how it is. I just needed to be by myself for a little bit. I want to talk to you about this." Taylor's watching us curiously from the top of the stairs, her head cocked to one side like she's trying to reason out an abstract painting at a museum. I lean into Evan and whisper so she can't hear me. "I want to talk to you, but not with *her* here."

He gives me this look. It's almost like I wounded him, but at the same time, he's too mad to be wounded.

"Oh, really?" he asks. "Is it not convenient for you right now? Geez, I'm so sorry. Why don't you let me know when you're in between one of your pity parties?" He looks at me so hard that it makes me press myself into the concrete wall that runs along the stairs. "Do you actually think you own the market on having sucky things happen to you? Do you think you're the only person who's mad about what happened? Because you're not. I'm mad. My mom's mad. My aunt's mad. And Taylor. What about her? And the other kids like her who got shot, and lived, but now have to look at their scars every day and remember what happened to them?"

I just stand there. It's so pathetic, but that's all I do. Because I know he's right.

"Let's go already!" Taylor calls from the top of the stairs.

Evan gives me one last look, then turns around. He takes the stairs two at a time. He's in a hurry to get to Taylor and away from me. He doesn't look back.

I can't stomach the idea of watching Evan and Taylor applying sunblock to each other, so I go inside.

I shut the door.

I sit at the computer.

I open a blank document.

I type the word *Dear*.

I watch my cursor blink.

Dear who? What do I need to say and to whom do I need to say it?

While I'm sitting there, staring at nothing, I hear Evan and Taylor leave. I picture Evan carrying his surfboard under his arm. I picture Taylor skipping after him. And what right do I have to care? He should be with someone who is willing to leave the house. I can picture their whole day outside. It will be perfect.

They will go to the beach. They will plop thick towels down in the warm sand. Evan will wax his board and Taylor will watch the muscles in his arms flex when he does it. The sight of that will make her swoon. She will comment on it. He will grin at her. That night, they'll watch the sun sink from the end of the pier. Evan will lean in and kiss her. They probably will have been kissing all day so they'll have a rhythm now. This will be their beginning.

And Taylor deserves that. She deserves to live every single minute of her life. She deserves to pull it behind her like a kite.

I envy that.

Why can't I be happy to be alive instead of afraid of living?

chapter twenty-five

"Hop on my back and I'll take you to the river," Ben says. He's sprawled out on his bed long after Evan and Taylor have gone surfing and then some. His hands are tucked behind his head.

I scan the page for my line. "But the river is so far, and it's getting dark."

"That's not how it goes. You're supposed to say: 'It's getting dark, and the river is too far.'"

"Geez, excuse me."

"It's supposed to be exactly right. That's what Ms. Belford said."

"Okay, start over."

Ben has memorized all his lines from the play along with everybody else's. I guess memorization is some great hidden talent of his. He recites his parts, and some of the extras, too, as we lie across from each other on our beds. I know most of the lines as well, so I try to take all the parts in between. When I stumble, Ben helps me to remember. It takes us almost an hour to get through the whole thing. When we're finished, I get up, turn off the light, and crawl back into bed. Ben rolls over to his side and flicks the switch on a new bedside lamp my mom won in a raffle at the hospital. It makes our room seem like it's underwater. Tiny yellow fish swim across the walls. I watch them move, around and around in circles, never really getting anywhere.

Ben speaks up when I thought he was practically asleep. His voice startles me. "You're coming to my play, right?"

I bury myself deeper into my sheets. "I hope so."

He sighs, and I can feel the weight of his exasperation in the air. A disappointed five-year-old is a brutal thing.

"But why wouldn't you go?" he asks. "What are you afraid of?"

What am I afraid of? *What if I throw up? What if I can't breathe? What if I get sweaty and have a panic attack and can't get out of the building? What if being in an auditorium reminds me of the last time I was near an auditorium?*

"I don't want to embarrass you," I say.

"It's okay if you clap the loudest. I won't be embarrassed. I want you to come."

"It's not that I don't want to be there. You get that, right?"

"All I know is if I wanna go somewhere, I go. You can, too."

My brother is too smart for his own good.

I remember reasoning out those exact same thoughts about my dad that time he didn't show up for Christmas almost a year and a half ago. I'd worked so hard putting together a scrapbook of the best moments my mom and Ben and I had shared over the past year without him. I thought he'd love it. But he didn't even show up. He wasn't in Afghanistan that Christmas. He was right down the coast. He could've been with us in a matter of hours. My mom had given him a chance to make things better. He could've been unwrapping the presents that Ben had made at preschool and diligently wrapped in tinfoil.

I thought he just didn't want to come.

I understand more now. I understand how my dad might've felt the same way I do at this moment. I understand how humiliating it is to see the look of disappointment on people's faces when they realize what you've become. My mom called back and forth with my grandma and my uncle Matt that Christmas day. She called because my dad had promised to spend the day with us. She called because she wanted to believe him, for my sake and for Ben's. But that was the night she stopped trying. That was the night she knew we had lost him for good. I knew it, too.

"This is what a promise from my dad looks like," I told my mom as she hung up the phone for the last time that day. "It looks like nothing."

I didn't say it in front of my brother. I'm not that mean. But I was angrier than I've ever been. How long will it be before Ben gets that mad at me? Will he stop bothering? I don't want to do that to him. And I don't want that to happen to us.

"I'm trying really hard," I tell Ben. "I want to be there. So much."

"Okay." He yawns and stretches his arms up over his head. "Then you will." The subject is closed for now. Somewhere, somehow, my little brother still believes in me.

It's only the first week of May. I still have time. I watch the fish swim and listen to Ben sink into sleep.

As I'm about to doze off myself, I hear the cell phone vibrate on Ben's nightstand. He must've taken it out of my drawer to play with it. I know it's Evan. I don't want to touch that phone. He can't possibly have anything nice to say. "Ben," I hiss through the fish. But Ben's sleeping soundly with his knuckles tucked under his chin and the collar of his dinosaur pajama top popped up to his earlobes. I get out of bed and grab the phone, telling myself I'll just shut it off and shove it back in the drawer without looking at what it says there.

But I'm a liar.

Evan's text is too bright, lighting up the screen in the middle of the night.

Evan: *You can return the phone since you refuse to use it. You probably won't even get this because I doubt you've turned it on.*

This is what he tells me. This is what he wants me to know.

After that, I can't sleep. I lie flat on my back and stare at the fish. The house is quiet until I hear my mom's footsteps in the hall. They are soft, barely perceptible. The deadbolt clicks free and the door creaks as she opens and shuts it. And then I hear her making her way down the concrete steps outside my bedroom window. It's late. She has to work in the morning. She can't possibly have somewhere to go. I pull aside my curtain, but I don't see her on the steps or in the courtyard. I tiptoe my way through the apartment. I peek through the crack of the door as I open it.

I still don't see her.

I step out onto the welcome mat and peer through the starry night. My eyes rake across the doors of each apartment.

They are shut.

The windows are dark.

The curtains are drawn.

The wind is gentle.

The moon is big.

The sound of the water licking the edges of the pool is all I can hear.

But then, in the midst of it all, I see her. My mom. She is in the far corner of the courtyard. She lies on a chaise longue. She smokes a cigarette. I've never seen my mom smoke a cigarette. I lean over the railing to peer down at her. I hear her then. She muffles a sob with the crook of her elbow, and I can see her body spasm as the emotions rip through her.

My mom is breaking down in the jasmine-scented courtyard of Paradise Manor on an almost-summer night.

She tries so hard, but she can't do it all. Tonight, I see what trying to do it all has done to her.

She looks up. She sees me watching. I've startled her. Her mouth drops open like she wants to explain, but she doesn't yell over to me. She swipes at her eyes. She crushes out her cigarette. She stretches her arms wide. She waits. It's an invitation. It's an asking. It's the admittance of her need to hold me. And for me to hold her.

I look at the door behind me. I've shut it like I never had any intention of going back inside. I look at the stairs in front of me. They don't seem that far. I take them, one by one, until I'm at the bottom. My mom is still waiting for me, arms outstretched, on that chaise longue across the courtyard. I don't think about what I'm doing anymore. I just go. I want to be what she needs. I pick up the pace. I need to get to her fast. I need to get to her before I can't.

I sink down on the chaise longue and into her. I curl up into a ball, and she hugs me. Her robe smells faintly of cigarette smoke, but more of laundry detergent. And the other smell of her is there, too. The smell that is my mom. It's a smell I can't explain, but it makes me feel safe and loved no matter what. She tucks my head under her chin and holds me tight. She holds me in.

And then we cry together, letting go of everything but each other.

chapter twenty-six

A week passes and Evan doesn't stop by. He doesn't knock. He doesn't call my name through the walls or the windows. He's finally done with me. I leave his phone by his doorstep when I know he's home. I knock and run back inside. It's for the best.

I am me. He is Evan. We are not an us.

Brenda seems disappointed. "What happened?" she asks.

"Everything changed when he showed up with Taylor."

"Who's Taylor?"

"I'm assuming she's his girlfriend. Love interest. Tandem surf buddy. Date to the prom. She's *something*."

"How do you know? Did you ask?"

"I didn't have to." Taylor had always been my biggest competition in the water, but now it's the same way on land. "I just know."

Brenda sighs. Annoyed. "Actually, you don't. You're making assumptions that aren't fair."

Is she serious right now? "Don't tell me about fair. Life isn't fair."

"No! It's not!" Brenda clenches her fists and slams them against her thighs in frustration with me. "Life's not fair, Morgan! But you know what? You're not being fair, either. It's not *fair* to shut people out who want to help. It's not fair to them. And it's not fair to you! You did the same thing with Evan you did with your friends. And where did that leave you? Alone. Do you want to be alone?"

"My friends are doing fine without me."

"How do you know? Did they tell you? Or are you assuming?" There's a sarcastic edge to her voice.

"Well, they don't come by to see me anymore. They're happy going to school and dances and parties and swim meets. They've all moved on just great, so I must be doing it wrong."

"They don't come by anymore because you pushed them away. If you push hard enough, eventually people will go!" She tosses her notebook onto the chaise longue next to her, plucks her hair back, and pinches the bridge of her nose between her thumb and index finger. She takes a deep breath, like she's going through her own checklist to calm down.

"Morgan." She sighs. "We aren't all wired in the same way. People grieve differently. Maybe what your friends are presenting on the outside is different from how they're feeling on the inside. Just because they seem okay doesn't mean they're not hurting in the same way you are."

"They couldn't possibly feel like I do."

"Why not? They were there, too. Sage was in the same building as you, for god's sake!"

"It was different for them than it was for me."

"Why? Tell me. How was it different for you?"

The words are so close. I can feel them in my throat. "It was raining that day."

"Yes, I know. You've told me that. Why is the rain so important?"

"It just is."

"Why?" Her question comes out like a whimper. Like she's exhausted. Like we've done this too many times.

"He wouldn't have gotten to school," I say.

"Who?"

"Him. Aaron. *Him*."

She sits up then. She heard me. She heard everything and then some. But she doesn't pick up her notebook yet. She's too busy paying attention to the fact that I've said something new.

"He wouldn't have gotten to school unless what?" she asks.

I put my face in my hands and scratch at my scalp. And then I grab chunks of my hair in my fists and pull. I think of the list taped to my wall inside. I might need it. Right now. Because I feel like I could throw up all over this chaise longue.

"Morgan." Brenda presses her hand to my wrist, stilling me. Stalling me. "What do you mean?"

I pull free from her grasp and stand up because the energy bubbling up inside of me makes it impossible to sit down anymore.

"I gave him a ride, okay?" I don't recognize my own voice. It's screechy and surreal. But I keep going because I have to. I started this. I'm finishing it. "He was walking in the rain and I saw him. He would've been late. We were too far from school to make it by first period. So I pulled over. I gave him a ride. I let him and his guns and every messed up thing about him into my car. I drove it all to school and dropped it off. I felt bad for him!"

Brenda can't help her reaction. "Oh, my god," she says, and her words make me so mad.

"*Oh, my god?* You don't get to say that!"

"You're right. That was very human of me. I'm sorry."

I look at her and I know she sees the truth of me in a way nobody else does. She understands me. That's why we've gotten this far. That's why I told her what I did. And I lose it because of her and all that she is and all that she's been to me. I'm suddenly snot and tears and wailing into the sunshine. And Brenda does one tiny thing. She reaches her hand out and knots her fingers with mine.

"Let it go," she says. "Just let it go."

chapter twenty-seven

My grandpa Ben took care of his car. He saved it for me. Sometimes grandparents feel the need to do things for their grandkids that their own children can't do. The car is basically an apology from my grandpa that my dad, his son, is the way he is. I was supposed to sell the Bel Air to help pay for college. But college isn't as alluring now that I can barely get through high school.

I can picture my grandpa with his car. My family didn't come from money, so that convertible was a really big deal. He told me how, as a teenager, he'd worked summers scrubbing barnacles off the bottoms of rowboats and school years mopping up puddles of grease at a local auto shop to save up enough money to buy it. He said it was just a Chevy at first. But as the years passed, it became a classic. He loved it like some people love their kids. He polished it to a blinding shine. He drove it up and down the coast on weekends. He showed it off at car festivals in beach towns and inland empires. He dropped the top. He hung one arm over the side of the door. He wore sunglasses and a baseball cap. Sometimes I went along.

He refused to pick up hitchhikers.

His car was the only thing he ever had that was worth anything. Now, it sits under a tarp in a parking space in the back of our building.

I used to love that car and the freedom it gave me to get around.

It's hard to believe there was a time when I couldn't stand the idea of being stuck inside. All I wanted was to be out in a world that was bigger and fuller than what I already knew. Eight months ago, in September, one month before October fifteenth, I drove the car to an away football game. Chelsea, Brianna, Sage, and I wore T-shirts we'd tie-dyed with our school's bright blue and orange colors. At the kitchen table at Brianna's house, we'd cut the bottoms into fringe and strung beads at the ends. We had ponytails with blue and orange ribbons and we chewed on red licorice vines and bubble gum. We matched. We had school spirit. We had dreams for the future.

We drove inland with the top down. We talked about boys we'd kissed and the text messages they'd sent that interrupted homework. There was a full moon and bright stars. Chelsea and Brianna sat in the backseat. Sage sat beside me. (Best friends always got dibs on the front seat.) And that night on the way to the football game, we sang along to an AM station because it was the only reception we could get. It was crunchy with static, but ripe with the kinds of pop songs where you know the words no matter what. You know them because they play them in the grocery store and on television commercials and in the juniors section of department stores.

A month later, everything changed.

I haven't wanted to be in the Bel Air since October fifteenth. Not since that morning that I saw Aaron Tiratore trudging through the rain.

I see him clearly in my mind. He walks down a wet sidewalk, his backpack hanging heavy over both his shoulders. The rain splats at his feet. His dark hair is matted wet against his head. I slow down because I think I know him. I think we had a math class together when I was a freshman. I feel bad letting someone walk to school in the rain, knowing they're going to be late because of it.

I pull over to the curb. I lean over to roll down the window. He stops. He stares.

"Want a ride?" I ask.

He twitches. He shrugs.

"Come on, you're getting soaked."

"Only if you're sure."

"I'm sure. Geez."

He gets in my car, trying to carefully settle his backpack between his feet, but it lands with a heavy thump that makes him do a double take. I didn't notice the sound then, but I hear it now. I hear it every day. It startled him. He picks the backpack up and sets it in his lap, holding it gently—the way I hold Ben during the scary parts of a movie.

I twist the dial for the heater, but only a halfhearted whir of warm air comes out.

"Sorry. Old cars are cool, but their heaters suck."

He doesn't answer. He doesn't look at me. He just looks out the window like nothing matters. I figure he's simply glad to be someplace that's dry. His jacket is a blue so bright that it almost hurts my eyes to look at it. It's thick and puffy, like a down comforter. It holds him in tight. It makes him look bigger than he is.

159

Aaron has bad skin. He smells gross, like old sweaty shoes. People make fun of him for the way he smells. People have always made fun of him. There's something achingly distant about him as he watches the world whiz by through the passenger side window.

"Thanks for the ride," he finally says. He doesn't look at me. He only says the words. "My bag is heavy."

He taps his fingers against his knee and doesn't stop.

"No problem."

I don't know what else to say to him. I don't know what Aaron does or what he likes or where he hangs out. I don't know if he has any friends. Practically everyone at school calls him "Wallpaper" because he's something that's there, but isn't particularly necessary. I know he isn't on the swim team, but I don't know whether he's on another sports team. I don't know if he hangs out at Clyde's Coffee on Friday nights like most people do. I don't know if he can read music or even what kind of music he likes to listen to. I don't know if he's ever kissed a girl. Or a boy. I don't know anything about him because I've never bothered to notice.

I fiddle with the radio dial because that's easier than talking and better than wondering. I settle on a morning sports program the radio was tuned to the day after my grandpa's funeral when my grandma handed me the keys to drive the car back to Pacific Palms.

Aaron says, "I've walked this same route to school for the last three years and nobody has ever stopped to give me a ride."

His words feel like something he's pulling from his mouth and handing over to me because he has to, not because he wants to.

"That sucks," I say.

"Yeah, well, it doesn't matter now."

I don't know what that means, but I'm turning into the parking lot so I don't bother to ask. I pull into a spot in the corner by the pool.

"Sorry. The walk to campus is farther from here, but I like having my car close when swim practice is over," I explain.

"No problem."

I pull a tube of lip gloss out from my jacket pocket and apply it. Aaron lifts up his heavy backpack and opens the door. He sets one foot down on the slick asphalt and scoots out. He stands up. Before he closes the door, he leans his head back into the car.

"Thanks again. That was a huge help," he says.

"No biggie. I'll pick you up whenever I see you from now on."

"Really? You would do that?"

"Yeah, why not? It's not like we aren't headed to the same place."

"Okay."

The rain pounds against the roof of the car. It hits the hood of Aaron's puffy blue jacket. Rivulets of water drip down from his backpack and splat on the ground.

"Go, you're getting soaked again."

"Yeah, you're right. I better get inside." But he doesn't pull his head out from the car right away. He wants to tell me something first. "You should wait out the rain here. I bet it'll stop by the end of first period."

He slams the door shut before I can tell him that I can't skip my English quiz. I watch him run across the parking lot and into the school. He's a flash of bright blue, the most obvious thing on campus, but not one person pays attention to him zipping past them.

chapter twenty-eight

After I finish my homework, watch two videotaped lectures for school, and mop and vacuum the floors, I sprawl out like a starfish on top of my bed to think. Yesterday, I told Brenda I gave Aaron a ride to school, and now I can't stop thinking about the letter I wrote to him. It's been sitting in the top drawer of my dresser for a month. I remember what I wrote, but I don't know how I said it. Or if I still mean my words in the same way. I take out the letter and stare at the address I got from the school directory and scrawled across the middle of the envelope. I rip the letter open. I read it through and cross stuff out. I add something else. I seal it back up in a fresh envelope. Before I can stop myself, I shove my feet into flip-flops, grab my keys, and head out the door.

I stomp down the stairs. I trample through the courtyard. I stumble past the pool. I reach for the front gate. But I stop. I sway. The rusted wrought iron taunts me; its rods hang heavy, like the bars of a prison cell. My palms sweat. The bile in my stomach churns.

I count to three.

I take deep breaths and watch the real world pass by.

A guy jogs by in running shorts. I can hear the bass-heavy beat of his music throbbing through his headphones. A lady bends over in work clothes and high heels to scoop up dog poop with a plastic baggie. Her Yorkie barks maniacally at a FedEx delivery guy balancing a package as big as his torso. Cars zoom past. *Zip, zip, zip.* A girl who looks my age rides by on her bike. The wind whips through her hair, and her loose shirt flutters out behind her like a cape.

It's life. All of it. Right here. Waiting for me. But it's moving so fast that it scares me. Things don't move this fast in my apartment, or even the courtyard of my apartment building.

Do I turn back around or keep moving?

Screw it. I'm going.

I visualized this sort of thing with Brenda. I can do it.

I yank the gate open. It's heavy and creaks with age. I pass through and let go of the handle. The heavy metal bangs shut behind me. I don't look back. I march down the sidewalk, moving with purpose past the people and the places and the things. Everything is normal. Everything is everyday. But I'm not. My brain is on overload. My head hurts from all the stimulation. And worry. I study the way a guy at the bus stop has his hands shoved into his pockets. Is he hiding something? I watch a girl with a weighed-down backpack. What's in there? A car runs a red light and another car honks. I jump. A guy on a skateboard whips past me, making me swirl around in a circle and into the safety of a nearby doorway. But I force myself to move again. I make my way down the block. I pass an apartment building almost identical to mine. I hear salsa music through an upstairs window. The beat of it thrums through my fingertips. It feels good. It's a hot day. And there, in the distance, I see it. A big blue mailbox. It's on the corner in front of the market where I used to buy Popsicles for Ben that would melt and drip down his arm in the sizzling summer sun. A few more feet. A few more squares of sidewalk. I'm almost there. My legs move underneath me like I'm not controlling them.

Until I get there.

I halt.

I pull open the drop box.

I shove my letter inside.

My fingers hold on to the edge of the envelope.

Until I let go.

I hear it plop against the other letters.

I pull my hand out.

The drop box bangs shut.

I walk away.

Realistically, what good is it? I can't get answers from a dead guy.

Dear Aaron,

Why did you do what you did? You changed me forever. Not because of what I saw or who you hurt, but because when you got into my car that day, you made me an accomplice. You made me a person who plays fifteen minutes of her life over and over again in her head. Why did I stop? Why did your bag make that noise? Why didn't you talk? Why did you tell me to wait? What did

I miss? ~~It's a horrible place to be. And for that, I hate~~
~~you. I. Hate. You.~~

   ~~I know you will never see this, but I needed to write~~
~~it. It needed to be said.~~

   ~~Morgan Grant~~

   But now I see that, sometimes, bad things bring people
together in ways we'd never imagine. I don't leave my
apartment, Aaron. I'm a shut-in. You made me afraid
of the world. It's May, and I haven't left where I live
in five and a half months. But after being alone in my
apartment for so long, I think there's a part of me that
understands how alone you felt. I'm sorry I didn't know.
I'm sorry you didn't have any friends or someone you
thought you could talk to. I'm sorry you thought you had
only one solution to your problems. I wish you'd gotten
help.

   I wish things hadn't happened the way they did.

   I want to hate you, but hating you has gotten me
nowhere. Forgiving you will start the healing. Forgiving
you will allow me to forgive myself.

   I know you will never see this, but I needed to write
it. It needed to be said.

   I forgive you.

                                        Sincerely,
                                        Morgan Grant

                        *   *   *

166

I run back home. I run because I want to endure the way my muscles protest. I want to feel the pounding of my heart in my chest. I want to hear the smack of my flip-flops on the sidewalk. I want to have the wind in my ears. I want to know the wind on my face.

When I get home again, I don't want to stop moving. I need to get this energy out somehow. I miss exercise. I miss the way it makes me feel. I want to stretch. I want to reach. I want to go. I want my body to be strong again.

I want to swim.

I peer out the window and down at the pool.

I let the curtain fall back into place.

I run through the apartment.

After a couple of rounds, I'm panting. I'm definitely out of shape. And having all the windows closed doesn't help. The stagnant inside air is stifling.

I head to the family room and open the window above the TV to let fresh air in. I flop down on the couch and flip through TV channels. I skip right past an exercise show from the eighties, then click back and watch, entranced. The workout host is wearing a shiny pink leotard and a yellow-and-white-striped terry cloth band around her forehead. Her hair is pulled back into a ponytail, but her bangs hang loose over the headband. She bounces from one foot to the other, pulling a knee toward her chest and touching it with her elbow. She looks like she's having a great time, and she sounds like she really wants everyone at home to join in.

"Get off the couch!" she shouts, as if she's talking right to me. "Today is the first day of the rest of your life!"

I bounce off the couch and start hopping around the room, mimicking her movements. I fear that I might look like a total oaf with no rhythm. Wearing jeans doesn't help. But I don't really care. Because moving is good. I can feel my heart working hard to keep up. I like that I'm winded and sucking in air. I love that I have sweat dripping down my back and collecting in the waistband of my underwear. My body is doing what it's supposed to do.

I'm alive.

The workout show is an hour long. There's a nice cooldown session at the end. I sit cross-legged on the floor and stretch. I can feel my muscles pull away from my rib cage as I reach my hand over my head and breathe out from my mouth. The cooldown part is kind of crunchy granola, and the host keeps telling all of us at home to stay centered.

"Be in the moment," she says. "This is your moment. There is only one you."

chapter twenty-nine

Ben comes busting through the door at six p.m. with my mom trailing behind him. I probably smell from my spontaneous eighties aerobics session a few hours ago, but nobody says anything. I press save on a persuasive essay about why cell phones should be allowed in school (uh, they're good in an emergency) and shut down the computer so I can focus on my brother. He's all excited because he got his costume for the play today. He yanks it out of his backpack with so much force that his lunch box and homework folder come toppling out, too. He waves his costume in front of my face. I pull it from his grasp so I can see it. It's just a green hoodie with giant googly eyes glued to the top to make it look like a frog. Ben thinks it's the greatest thing ever.

"It's awesome," I say, holding it up to him. "Try it on. I wanna see."

Ben pulls the sweatshirt over his head and the googly eyes roll back and forth, landing cross-eyed. "Do you like it?"

"I think it's pretty much the best costume I've ever seen. And you're the best frog in the history of frogs."

He grins up at me and the googly eyes roll back. I pull the sweatshirt off him even though he begs me to let him wear it through dinner.

"What if you get spaghetti sauce all over it? What frog eats spaghetti? That stain wouldn't even make sense."

"Yeah, that's true," he says, even though I can tell he's not entirely convinced that a spaghetti-eating frog wouldn't be totally cool.

When we sit down to eat, Ben launches into his usual play-by-play of his whole day at school. Today was library day, so he picked out a bunch of books he wants to read together before bed.

"I got one with a mermaid in it because she looks like you," he says.

My mom smiles and points at the side of her mouth with her fork to let Ben know he has some stray sauce to wipe up. He grabs his napkin from his lap and swipes it across his messy face.

"Your grandma checked in today," my mom says, looking at me. I can tell she's trying to sound casual so Ben doesn't pick up on any weird vibes.

"Any news?"

"Nothing." My mom shakes her head. Tired. Resigned.

That means nobody has heard from my dad since he took off with his bag full of new clothes and my grandma's jewelry.

"Maybe it's for the best," I say.

"Perhaps."

After I've showered and read the mermaid book to Ben three times in a row, I crawl into my own bed. Outside, the front gate of Paradise Manor bangs shut. I can hear Evan. I recognize his voice. He's talking on his phone in the courtyard. I peek out from my curtain just as he's heading up the stairs in front of my bedroom window. I hadn't realized he was *that* close. I freeze when he actually sees me. He stops, stunned, in the middle of the stairs to observe me through the window. We only make eye contact. Silent. I wave, and he waves back. Halfhearted. I let go of the curtain. It falls back into place, and Evan disappears behind it.

chapter thirty

Today, May twenty-third, is Ben's birthday, so when Brenda arrives, I suggest we walk to the corner market to buy a cake mix and a tub of frosting with the money I still have saved up from teaching swim lessons. We've had two sessions since I told Brenda I gave Aaron a ride to school on October fifteenth, and she doesn't stop to stare at me for even one second this afternoon when I say I want to leave Paradise Manor.

"Let's go," she says, so I follow her down the stairs and out the front gate.

The sidewalk seems less busy than when I mailed Aaron's letter last week. Or less shocking. It just feels like I'm supposed to be walking here. The world is everywhere and it's even better to be out in it with someone next to me. And even though I like Brenda, right now I kind of wish she were Evan. The thought surprises me. I've been trying not to think of him since he cut me out of his life.

"How are you feeling? We've had a lot to cover in our last sessions."

I guess we're going to walk and talk about things that matter as we go. I squint through the brightness of the afternoon to look at her, wishing I'd remembered my sunglasses.

"I feel good. Like I can breathe again."

"How so?"

I spent the last two sessions telling Brenda everything about those fifteen minutes I drove in my car with Aaron. I told her about his bulky backpack and the way he smelled. I told her the things he said and the things I wished I could take back.

"Well, you know that saying about having the weight of the world on your shoulders?"

Brenda nods. The force of a Santa Ana wind whips past us, making my frizzy hair flat, and I brace myself against it.

"I didn't really know what that meant until I felt that way."

"And how do you feel now?"

I think for a minute. "This might sound really weird, but it makes me think of my team suit. For swimming. It's tight. And sometimes it crushes my chest a little. Still, it's the uniform and it makes me go faster and I'm required to wear it to compete. Yet sometimes, after a meet, it just feels so good to take it off."

Brenda nods.

"Even though it's off, there are still marks on my skin where the straps have dug in. Or I'm chafed under my armpits. So it almost feels like I'm still wearing it. I'm still kind of uncomfortable."

"I understand what you're trying to say."

"Will it get better?" My fingers flutter at my sides like an instantaneous reaction to that fear. "Like, what if I cross the street tomorrow and it's one block too many? Will I freak out and have to start all over again?"

I should probably let Brenda know I left my apartment by myself last week, but that would mean telling her I wrote a letter to

Aaron. She might not like that I wrote another letter and didn't let her read it. I figured since Aaron is dead, it didn't matter if I mailed it or not. I wrote it because I had to. I wrote it and it made me feel better. I mailed it because I wanted to let go.

"You're testing boundaries," Brenda says. "Your day-to-day is going to be less about overcoming and more about managing."

She waits for me to punch the button for the crosswalk.

"Morgan, what you admitted—about giving Aaron a ride to school—that was profound. You need to process it. You need to fully work through the emotions of that. I can see that you're trying. And I know how hard it is. But saying it out loud was important. Admitting it was a huge step. As long as you keep doing what you're doing, you're going to keep moving forward."

There are people and cars all around us, but she doesn't even seem to notice because she's too busy making eye contact with me. She seems like she understands so much that it makes me wonder if there's something she's had to carry around her whole life, too.

"But maybe," I say, "if I hadn't given Aaron a ride to school, he wouldn't have done what he did."

Brenda stops in the middle of the sidewalk. "I want you to hear this because it's important, got it?"

"Yeah."

"It's okay that you gave Aaron a ride. The fact that you gave him a ride didn't make a difference. He was going to get to school and do what he did whether you picked him up or not. Do you understand that?"

"How do you know?"

"Because when someone like Aaron is set on doing something, he's going to find a way no matter what."

There's a bus stop bench nearby, and I motion to it. I want to stay there and just breathe. Brenda sits next to me. We look out at the street. We watch the traffic.

Brenda says, "It's a lot to take in, I know."

I nod. The wind is there. And the street. And the people. And the cars. I listen. I breathe. I think. I process. I've spent minutes, hours, weeks, and months thinking I could've made a difference if I hadn't stopped to give him a ride. Or if I'd picked up on the clues that are so clear to me now. His backpack. His warning to skip first period. Everything he said. But if I believe what Brenda is telling me, I couldn't have changed the outcome. Not at all.

"Don't punish yourself for being kind," Brenda says. "Perhaps more people should've been kind to Aaron."

When I'm ready, we head inside the corner store. The smell of deli sandwiches crawls up my nostrils, making my mouth water. I remember roast beef on sourdough bread and sour cream and onion potato chips. I remember getting food to go on Saturdays in the summer and eating it on the beach with Sage while we watched the waves roll in. I suddenly want a roast beef sandwich because I can have a roast beef sandwich. I'm sick of grilled cheese.

I cross over to the deli counter. Brenda follows me. She's observing, not talking. I place my order, and the girl behind the counter rips off the bottom portion of the order ticket, writes the price on it, and hands it to me. I grip it between my fingertips as

I cruise the aisles looking for baking supplies. Brenda is still there. She's with me, but quiet. There are a few dusty boxes of cake mix on a shelf near the back freezer.

"I don't think people come here very often for birthday cake," I say. I check the expiration dates on the frosting and the cake mix, settling on the one that expires in three months instead of three weeks.

I tap out all my funds paying for my sandwich and cake supplies. We leave, making our way back out to the pockmarked sidewalks of my town. I glance at the mailbox in front of me. I think of my letter and wonder if it has made its way across town yet. Brenda and I traipse past it, dodging a guy on a bike. The sudden swoosh of him makes me jump, and my heart speeds up.

When we get back to my house, Brenda comes inside and I put my sandwich in the refrigerator for later. Brenda settles on a stool at the counter to watch me stir chocolate cake mix, eggs, and vegetable oil with a big wooden spoon. She asks me some questions, simple stuff about how I plan to decorate the cake and what sort of celebration we're planning. I answer her while dumping the mix into a baking dish coated with cooking spray. When it's time to go, she gives me a hug. She's never done that before. It's not creepy or anything. It's just different. But it's meaningful, too. It's like her way of saying she's happy with what I'm becoming.

"Thank you for everything you do," I tell her.

"I'm happy to do it. You've helped me, too."

"I have? How?"

She takes in a deep breath, closing her eyes. "We have more in common than you know. I'm just glad I can be here for you."

I hug her because that's all I want to do. It's the only response I have.

"Ben's going to love the cake," she says as we pull away from each other.

She smiles at me, and I think it's weird how I might be helping her, too.

chapter thirty-one

My mom is relieved I baked a cake, because we'd be up hours past Ben's bedtime if she had to bake one herself. Still, she wants to know how I got the ingredients.

"Brenda and I took a field trip," I explain. "We walked to the market on the corner."

"Morgan, that's huge." She holds my face in her hands. She kisses my forehead. "I'm so proud of you. I knew you could do it."

I nod. I'm glad she's proud, but I don't want to keep talking about it.

Ben loves my cake. I used chocolate frosting and sprinkled brown sugar on top to look like dirt. Then I took some of Ben's plastic dinosaurs and plunked them down on top of the brown sugar. My brother blows out the candles, then picks up each of the dinosaurs to lick the frosting from their feet. I reassure my mom that I washed all of them when she cringes in disgust.

I cut slices of cake and slide them over to my mom and Ben at the counter. I stand in the kitchen to eat mine.

Through a forkful of cake, Ben asks if we can play Go Fish after he takes his bath.

"Dude, it's your birthday. We can pretty much do whatever you want," I say.

"Really?"

He gets this look on his face like he's thinking really hard about what he wants to do. I wait for him to ask for something over-the-top, like going for a ride on the old wooden roller coaster by the beach, but he doesn't say it.

"I wanna give Evan some cake," he says. "Can he come over?"

My mom looks at me over her plate, with her eyebrows raised like, *Well, can he?*

"No way," I say. "That's not a good idea."

Ben slumps down on his stool, resting his chin on the counter. I'm a horrible sister to project my issues onto my little brother's birthday celebration. But how can I sit here eating cake with Evan when he doesn't even want to talk to me?

My mom butts in. "I think it would be really nice to invite Evan over for a piece of cake."

Ben is off his stool and out the front door before I even come close to grabbing him by the collar of his shirt. The next thing I know, Evan's shuffling sheepishly through our apartment in board shorts and a faded thermal. He takes a seat at the counter between Ben and my "Calm Down and Get It Together" checklist. I'm still in the kitchen so he stares me down through the space between the counter and the overhead cabinets.

"Hey," he says, nodding at me.

"Hi."

"Can I have a piece with dirt on it?" he asks.

This request sends Ben into a fit of giggles. "It's just brown sugar."

"It is? Bummer. I wanted real dirt," Evan says.

Ben snort-laughs, choking on his milk for a second so that Evan has to pound his back and ask if he's okay. Ben chills out, and my mom tells Evan his mom should come over, too.

"I'm sure she'd love to, but she's at my aunt's," he says through a mouthful of cake. He looks at Ben. "It's too bad, because she loves cake with dirt on it."

Again, Ben snort-laughs.

"Who doesn't love cake with dirt on it?" I ask, trying to keep up the momentum.

Evan jerks his head in my direction. "Whoa! You speak! I forgot what you sounded like."

Yeah, right. Like he even cares.

"She sounds like this: *wah wah wah wah wah*," Ben says.

"I do not sound like that!"

My mom stands up like she just received some offstage cue to busy herself in the kitchen. Ben sits there, oblivious, shoveling cake into his mouth. My mom opens a drawer. She rips off a ream of tinfoil. She covers the cake. She turns on the faucet. She rinses pots and pans from dinner. We had macaroni and cheese with a side of mashed potatoes because Ben got to pick. I'm going to have to do a double eighties aerobics workout tomorrow to make up for this meal.

Evan and I watch each other, wondering who will talk next. I'm sick of cake, but I keep eating because it gives me something to do.

"Do I really sound like that?" I finally ask Evan.

"No." He tosses a lopsided grin my way. "It's actually more screechy."

I open my mouth to tell him off, but I can see that his lips are bunched up, holding in a laugh. I don't know why it is that whenever he's in my apartment everything seems less dark.

"Very funny," I say. "Seriously. You're hilarious."

"Thanks. I know."

My mom finishes up and nudges me out of the kitchen by tapping her hip to mine. "How about we open presents?" she says, throwing her hands up in the air like she's about to start a conga line.

Ben jumps up and down because he's officially six and presents are the best thing in the world when you're six. My mom goes back to the bedroom to grab the gifts, and Evan and I settle on our respective ends of the couch. Ben sits in the middle of the floor waiting for my mom to hand the presents over. She returns with a couple of gifts and whips out her camera to take pictures as we watch Ben rip dinosaur-print wrapping paper off boxes like it's a sport. My mom got him new Vans and an at-home science experiment kit. When he tears into the cardboard lining of the kit, she stops him.

"Outside," she tells him. "In daylight. I can't have you burning down Paradise Manor."

I hand Ben a card I made. I drew a picture of him riding an apatosaurus and stuffed ten bucks of my own birthday money from September inside the card. "Save it," I tell him.

He nods. "Can we check the mail?" He pops up and riffles through the pile of envelopes on the counter. "I bet I got more." He pulls an envelope free from between the coupon mailers and bills. "See? Here's one."

"You're very popular," I say.

Ben rips the envelope open. His forehead crinkles up as he reads the words on the front. "I don't get it."

I pull it from his hands and read it to myself. *In Deepest Sympathy* it says. But it's been crossed out with green pen and *Happy Birthday* has been scrawled underneath it in the barely legible chicken scratch I recognize immediately.

"It's from Dad," I say.

The whole room goes stiff. My dad isn't here, but he's still managing to make us feel as edgy as if he were sitting on the couch watching us through drunk eyes. And at the same time, even though I know it'll only set me up for disappointment, there's this sliver of longing. Of hope. It hits me at the core. I can see the expression on my mom's face and on Ben's. I know they're thinking the same thing: Did he change? Is he better? Does he still love us? But no.

"What does it say?" Ben asks, all eager.

I open the card up and read out loud. *"Happy Birthday, Benjamin. See you soon. Love, Dad."*

My mom is silent. Evan is, too. I want to throw up.

"See you soon, my ass," I mutter under my breath, tossing the card to Ben like a Frisbee.

"Well, that was fun," my mom says. She bends down to gather all the wayward wrapping paper and envelopes into a pile on the floor. "Time for your bath, Ben."

Evan high-fives my brother, and then Ben races down the hallway to the bathroom. "I owe you a present," Evan calls out to him.

My mom follows Ben. I pick up the wrapping paper and dump it into the trash can labeled for recycling. It's full so I punch it down, deflating orange juice and milk cartons in the process. I pummel the pile until it settles into half the size of what it used to be.

I punch it and punch it again.

Evan's fingertips brush my shoulder. I feel the heat of his fingers through my T-shirt.

"Hey. Are you all right?" he asks.

I push out from under him. "You don't have to be nice to me."

"I know. But I'm doing it anyway. I must be a glutton for punishment."

I turn to look at him. "Why does my dad have to be like that?"

"I'm the wrong person to ask. My dad's not all that great himself."

Before I burst into a full-on sob, Evan pulls me to him. He grips me tight into a bear hug and rests his chin on top of my head. It's such a relief. He smells like a mixture of sunblock and surf wax. We sway. His golden-tipped curls mix into my own hair and I breathe him in, wishing I didn't have to let go of him again.

"Thanks," I tell him. My voice is muffled against his chest and his shirt. "Tomorrow you can go back to not talking to me."

He doesn't say anything. He just grips me tighter, like he doesn't want to let go, either.

Once I've calmed down, he tilts my chin up to see him. "I need you to wait here. Can you wait right here? For just a second?"

I shrug my shoulders. "Where else am I going to go?"

He laughs. "I think you might surprise yourself."

Evan darts over to his apartment and comes back a minute later holding a canvas. It's a pretty decent size, big like the ones we used in art class. He turns it around so I can see what's painted on it.

It's me.

Only it's not me the way I am now. It's me the way I was before. Vibrant. Alive.

I take a step back. "How did you . . . Who painted that?" I ask.

"Don't freak out, okay?"

"Should I freak out?"

"Connor painted it."

"What? When?"

He shrugs. "Last year. This is what he did. He painted portraits of people he cared about. Everyone in my family has one. I thought you should have yours. I've wanted to give it to you for a long time, but I didn't want to weird you out."

I take the canvas from him and study it. It's surreal to see someone else's version of me so big. And flawless. Am I supposed to hang this in my room and stare at it? "Well, now I guess you know what I used to look like."

"What're you talking about?"

"This painting is obviously a totally idealized version of me."

"You're hardly unattractive, Morgan."

"I'm hardly like this," I say, gesturing to the painting.

"No, you're better."

"Oh, really? How so?"

He sighs. "For the record, I don't think you give yourself enough credit. First of all, you aren't ugly, so please stop saying that. You're smart. And most of all, you're real. Everything you've been through, and the way you're trying to work through it, actually makes you *more* attractive. To me. But you're so busy trying to convince me of all the reasons people *shouldn't* like you that you can't even see people *do* like you."

I think about that for a minute. Silently studying Evan and the way he's silently studying me.

"*I* like you," he says.

"I like you, too."

chapter thirty-two

I see Aaron Tiratore in my dreams. Brenda knows. We've talked about it. She told me I should write my dreams down. I have bits and pieces of them on crinkled pieces of paper that I've shoved into the bottom of a drawer. Others, I ripped to shreds and dumped in the trash.

In my dreams, I never know what kind of mood Aaron will be in. Sometimes he's mad. Other times he's my best friend. Usually, he changes his mood in the middle of a thought. But always, we're in the hallway by the auditorium. In the alcove. It's the last place I saw him. And every time we meet, I try to stop him.

I dream of him tonight.

On Ben's birthday.

In my dream, I'm running. I toss aside blankets and kick off sheets.

I run so fast. We all do. We slam through doors and tear down hallways. Some people go this direction. Some people go that one. We all try to find a way out. We all try to find a place to hide that will only be ours. Some of us make it. Some of us don't. One person falls to the ground right next to me as Aaron storms through classrooms and corridors. The principal yells over the loudspeaker that we are on lockdown. We are supposed to be huddled under desks and behind bolted doors, with the lights shut off, like we repeatedly practiced in school safety drills. But so many of us are running. So many of us are trying to get out. I hear screaming in the distance. I hear screaming right in front of me.

I run and run.

And then I wake up.

I'm drenched in sweat. I think Aaron is here for real. In my apartment. I swear I hear his boots on the ground. Down the hall. I'm ready to scream until I realize Ben is breathing in the bed across from me. His green frog sweatshirt hangs from the bedpost, looking at me cross-eyed. My painting is propped up on my dresser even though it seems weird to have it there.

I scrub at my eyes, trying to stop the flood of memories that won't stop. But they're here now. They want me to see them.

And so I do.

It becomes that day.

I run to my secret spot. It's a tiny alcove tucked into the end of the hallway by the auditorium. It's where I went last spring when I found out Taylor Schneider was named sophomore swim team captain instead of me. It's where I went when I needed to study for a math test and the cafeteria was too loud. Now, it's where I go to try to stay alive.

I cower in a ball. I hope I won't hear anyone coming after me. In that alcove, I put my hands on top of my head. I rock. I feel exposed even though I've gone to the best place I know to hide. Static bits of my life weave a staccato rhythm through my brain. I picture Ben being born. I see fluorescent lights and the smile of the nurse before she laid him on my mom's chest. I hear my mom's laugh. I see her happy tears. I feel my tears, too. I watch Ben's red face pucker up and scream. I remember my grandpa Ben. I hug him tight. I smell dinner cooking. I smell wet grass. I smell chlorine. I feel the water of the swimming pool through my fingers. I dive under a wave. I grab a handful of sand. I roll a snowball with fingers stuffed into bright red mittens. I feel the wind in my hair. I kiss someone who matters. I hold on.

I wish for a happy ending.

I hope whoever is doing this will pass me by. That they'll turn down another hallway that leads right out of the school and into the back of a police car.

But that's not what happens.

Instead, everything stops.

It's hard to breathe.

I hear the whisper-thin scratch of him.

He's standing to the left of me.

Blocking me in.

I hear myself crying.

"Look at me!" he shouts.

His eyes are wild. He's nothing like the person who sat in my car an hour ago. He's not withdrawn. He's in a moment that is only his. His puffy blue jacket is spattered with blood. He has a cut on his face. He's wearing combat boots like the ones my dad wore in Afghanistan. Like the ones lined up in our closet when he returned home.

But Aaron's not a hero.

He whips his gun around. He holds it to my head.

I look at him.

And then he freezes like he sees me and who I am. It's as if a flash of a memory zipped through his brain and jolted him from his stupor. And all I can do is hope that it means something.

"Please don't," I whimper. "Please."

He puts his hand to his ear and motions for me to listen. "Do you hear that? Sirens. They're coming." His voice is faraway and dreamy, like he's remembering a family vacation or building a fort as a kid. Like he's thinking of waterslides and chocolate-dipped ice-cream cones. "It won't be long now."

He looks at me like he wants me to say something back, so I nod. The tip of his gun presses hard against my forehead when I do it.

I wish my life had been better.

I wish I were leaving something significant behind.

I close my eyes tight because I don't want Aaron's eyes to be the last things I see.

"There's a part of me that wanted you to figure it out," he says, tapping his fingertips to my chin, forcing me to open my eyes and see him.

His gun is on my forehead. I'm waiting.

"I'm sorry," he says.

I wait still. Crying. Begging.

And then Aaron abruptly pulls the gun away from my head, shoves the tip of it into his mouth, and shoots.

*   *   *

I have to remind myself that it isn't happening right now. It did happen. On October fifteenth. But today is May twenty-third, seven months later. I'm in my apartment, far away from school. And the alcove. And Aaron. And his gun.

I consider waking up my mom.

I won't.

I think of my emergency pills and whether or not I need one.

I don't.

I sink back into my pillow and stare at the ceiling.

I listen to Ben breathe through the dark.

I wonder what he dreams.

After October fifteenth, after that day, everyone wanted answers. Before Aaron's Facebook page was disabled, news outlets released photographs from his profile. They found the worst ones. The ones that painted the picture of a kid who was angry and alone. They interviewed neighbors who said Aaron spent weekends tinkering in the garage. His mom revealed Aaron had been in therapy since middle school. His dad revealed he kept guns in the house. For protection. From the world. Not from his son. Those were the guns Aaron brought to school on October fifteenth.

"Aaron was a loner. He kept to himself," a classmate said in front of the makeshift memorial at PPHS. It was night and dark and she held a candle that dripped wax into the tiny paper plate surrounding it, the edges flipped up like a summer skirt.

The school choir sang sad songs.

Students wept.

Parents hugged.

And the only person who could give us answers, who could tell us why, was gone.

I never told anybody until Brenda that I'd given Aaron a ride to school on October fifteenth. But I did tell the police Aaron had killed himself in front of me. I told them when I was in the separate language arts building line on the football field. I said I was the last person to see him. That's why I had to go to the police station. They hoped I'd have answers I didn't have.

chapter thirty-three

Summer is almost here. The air is telling me so. Evan went to the desert with his mom for the Memorial Day weekend, and I haven't heard him or seen him or breathed the ocean smell of him since Ben's birthday.

"I've never been to the desert. I heard it's unbearably hot. Will I melt?" Evan asked Ben when he left our apartment that night with a giant slice of dinosaur birthday cake for his mom.

"Just watch out for rattlesnakes," Ben warned him. "They come out at night."

And now it's Wednesday and Ben and Evan are back at school. My mom is at work. By the afternoon, the inside of my apartment is so hot, I can hardly breathe. I slide the bedroom window open and sit in the fresh air that comes through the screen. I've got my notebook propped on my lap and thoughts in my head. I'm writing down things I remember from years ago. I remember when Ben was small and I was bold. I recall wildfire warnings. I remember the way ash blew down from the foothills and into the courtyard of Paradise Manor two Septembers ago. There was the smell of smoke in the air and the burn of it in my lungs and my eyes. Sunsets blistered the sky in pink and orange. I stood at the edge of the swimming pool and scooped out ash, dumping it into a pile next to my bare feet. I scooped out the ash because it was a hot day and I wanted to swim.

That same heat is here this afternoon, minus the smoke.

My hair sticks to my forehead. My underarms stink.

I think of the pool downstairs. I could jump right in right now. I would cool off in no time. I make the choice. I leap off my bed and pull off my clothes. I yank my team suit from the door handle where it's been taunting me for months. I slide it on. The good thing about Speedos is that they stretch. My suit effortlessly sucks up the pounds I still need to lose. I grab my goggles and race down the hall and out the door. Barefoot in my bathing suit.

The turquoise water winks at me.

It licks a come-hither message at the edges.

I skitter down the stairs. I stop shy of the pool. I back up to the front gate. I take a running start.

I leap.

For a split second, I fly through the air. My feet hit first. The splash echoes through the courtyard. My body sinks downward in follow-through. Oh, the pure bliss of cool water and chlorine.

In my hair.

On my skin.

Through my fingertips.

I rise to the surface and kick my feet, blasting through the water and gulping in air. I climb out and scoop the leaves from the surface of the pool. There aren't many of them. I think Evan has been busy with the upkeep. I jump back in when I'm done.

The pool is small, but I take long, even strokes, propelling back and forth, wall to wall. I'm weightless. I'm free. I'm where I'm meant to be. People either are or are not of the water. It either means something to them or it doesn't. I know in this moment that I'm not myself without it. I know this as much as I know anything. My need is palpable.

I swim. I float. I breathe. I burn. I hope. I dream. I think. I wonder. I am.

I think of Evan in the ocean and on his surfboard. I think of him loving the water as much as I do.

And then I sink to the bottom of the pool.

My hair floats out around me. I hold my breath. My goggles make everything crystal clear, from the crack in the bright blue tile mosaic in the deep end to the leaf stuck in the drain. I let out the air from my lungs slowly, watching tiny bubbles rise to the surface.

Blip, blip, blip.

Pop, pop, pop.

I'm watching. I'm waiting. I'm about to rise up again when the water suddenly jostles me. Someone else has jumped in. They yank me from behind, holding me tight so I can't move as they pull me up and through the surface. I scream and flail, splashing water everywhere with my feet. My brain is about to go into full-blown panic mode.

"What the hell?" I yell, punching at nothing because whoever is holding me is gripping me so tightly that my hands are about as effective as the forelimbs on a Tyrannosaurus rex in one of Ben's dinosaur books.

"What are you doing?" Freaking Evan.

"What are *you* doing? Let go of me! I don't need saving!"

We hit the waist-high water of the shallow end and Evan lets me go. He's fully clothed. His hair is dripping, and a bright green T-shirt advertising a Hawaiian shave ice shop clings to him. I push him hard. Even though we're only waist-deep, he rocks back on his feet despite the fact that he's so big and brawny.

"I'm sorry," he says. "I thought maybe you were doing something stupid."

"I'm not stupid!"

"I didn't say you *were* stupid. I said I thought you might be *doing* something stupid."

Underwater, I curl my hands into fists like Ben does when my mom tells him he can't watch a TV show past his bedtime. "That's the same thing!"

Evan pushes his hair back from his face and water droplets fly off the curly ends and land in the pool. "I thought you were drowning, okay? I thought I was helping you. I'm sorry."

He looks sincerely apologetic, with his big brown eyes bewildered. But I'm too mad to care. Okay, maybe I care a little bit.

I rip off my goggles and toss them onto the pool deck. They skip then skid. I point at my Speedo. "Hello? Swimming here. Kind of a big deal for me."

"You weren't swimming. You were sitting at the bottom of the pool doing nothing. I thought you were drowning."

"I was thinking!"

"Well, stop thinking!"

"How am I supposed to do that?"

He's poised to yell again. He opens his mouth to let loose. But then he clamps it shut. He smacks at the surface of the pool because we're still standing in the shallow end. Drops of water fly up into the air and splash back down again. I roll my eyes. He rolls his back.

Eye-roll challenge.

He crosses his arms over his chest, all huffing and puffing and blowing my house down. I try to muffle a laugh, but it spits out of my mouth and breaks through the courtyard.

"What's so funny?" he asks.

I try to be serious, but when I look at him, I know my eyes are cracking up. "You jumped in with your clothes on," I say.

"Yeah? So what?"

"That's so dramatic," I mutter. "I was just *thinking*."

"There are better places to think, you know?"

"I used to do all my thinking underwater."

He leans back on his elbows against the edge of the pool, shifting to casual, like we're suddenly at some fancy resort where people order drinks with tiny umbrellas in them.

"Okay, so what were you thinking about that was so important?"

"I don't know. Stuff."

"Like what?"

Who is he? Brenda? "Like that it felt good to be back in the pool." Since Evan is of the water, he will understand what I mean.

"Yeah?"

"Yeah."

"That's good."

He reaches out his hand. He flutters his fingers in the pool, daring me to take them. I reach out to him, only my fingertips at first. Then he grabs my hand to knot our fingers together just under the surface.

"What else?" he asks.

"Nothing." I look at our hands before I look at him. "Maybe you a little."

"I like that." He pulls me closer to him. I look up. He looks down, pushing my wet hair back from my face. "But only a little?"

I nod.

"I wish you thought about me more than a little," he says. "I think about you more than a little."

I flutter in my heart and in my hands. "I might think about you more than a little. If I'm being honest."

"Yeah?"

I nod again. "But I shouldn't because of Taylor."

"Taylor? What? Why?"

"Aren't you guys a thing?"

"Whoa. Not even. We just hang out. And surf."

He leans in, bit by bit. Close enough to make me suck in a breath.

"Really?"

He grins. "I swear."

"So you're glad that I think about you?"

He nods.

"And you think about me?"

He nods again.

"Okay."

He leans in a little more. And I wait. He slows down for only a second. Until he finally presses his mouth to mine. We're all soft lips and pool water until suddenly we're not. We quickly become swoony thoughts and grabby hands. We're clumsy and giggling until off in the distance someone whistles and claps.

"Woo-hoo! Get some!" they yell.

I break away from Evan to look over his shoulder and see Taylor standing by the mailboxes. Her camouflage tank top and black workout pants are drenched in pink, yellow, and pale blue paint, while her arm muscles bulge out as buff as G. I. Jane's.

"I knew it," she squeaks. "God, I love love."

I raise an eyebrow at Evan. "Do the two of you have plans to hang out and surf today?"

"No. But I'd cancel if we did," Evan says, ducking into me again.

I laugh, wrestling myself away. "Taylor's right there. She'll see us."

"So what? I don't care if the whole world sees us."

"Seriously, Morgan. I've seen it all," Taylor says, sauntering over. "Actually, I've *done* it all." She waves us away with her hand like we're as insignificant as spare change in the tip jar at Starbucks. "You guys being happy makes me happy, so carry on." She sinks onto a chaise longue, leans back, and closes her eyes to the sun, making it easy to study her.

"Why are you covered in all that gunk?" I ask.

"Paintball. It's my new thing."

What? Is she serious? I pull myself out of the pool and hover at her feet, dripping water on her toes. "Paintball? Sorry, Taylor, but that is kind of messed up."

She shades her face with her hand to look up at me. "Not really. At least with paintball, I have a gun, too." She smiles, leans back, and shuts her eyes again.

Evan comes up behind me. We stand. We stare. We drip water onto the pool deck. I lean into him and whisper, "Is she okay?"

He shrugs. "In her own way, yeah."

I look at Taylor, all long limbs, taut muscles, and tan skin. She's completely oblivious to the fact that I'm trying so hard to figure out this new version of her.

"I'm going to get a towel," I finally say. In my hurry to get to the pool, I forgot one.

"I'll be right here." Taylor doesn't bother to open her eyes or move. "I just came by to say hi, but you guys are clearly busy. I'm good just hanging in the sun until I have to go to the gym. Toss down a trashy celeb mag if you have one."

Evan follows me up the stairs and stops me at my door. He leans into me, and I have to grab handfuls of his shirt to keep my balance.

"So it's okay that I kissed you?" he asks.

"Yeah, it's fine." I fumble awkwardly, shifting from foot to foot.

"And I can give the cell phone back to you?"

I nod.

"And you'll answer my texts?"

"Yes."

He leans down until his lips are so close to my ear that my nerves get zippy. "Thank you," he whispers.

He kisses the shell of my ear, and I'm suddenly fully aware that

I'm in a wet, clingy bathing suit and Evan isn't. His fingertips press into the bare skin of my back, pulling me closer to him. I grip the edges of his soaked shirt. I hold on tight. He plants butterfly kisses from my chin to my cheek, stopping at my mouth. He looks at me, his eyes asking me if it's okay. I nod and kiss him first.

chapter thirty-four

By the time my mom gets home, Taylor is long gone, off to some class at the gym to build muscles even bigger than the ones she already has. Since then, Evan and I have gone from not doing homework to doing homework. My mom asks him to stay for dinner. He says yes before she even has all the words out. He seems to like hanging out in our apartment. Maybe it's because his mom is gone so much. That must suck. I'm by myself most of the time, too, but at least I know I'll get to have dinner with my mom and Ben at the end of the day.

My mom makes pasta with pesto sauce and I make a salad. Ben and Evan are in charge of the garlic bread, so some of it comes out charred, but not awful. We eat the way we always do— me on the kitchen side of the counter and my mom and Ben across from me. Evan has his own spot now, too, on the stool between Ben and my calm-down checklist.

We talk about things that matter and things that don't. My mom asks Evan if he likes living in Pacific Palms.

"I don't hate it," he says, smiling at me.

After dinner, we all take parts in Ben's play and recite them out loud. The performance is in a week and a half, and Ben brought home tickets he made in class. He even brought one for Evan. When he hands it over, Evan leans in to me and whispers, "It can be our first date. The theater. So highbrow."

My heart thunders and my stomach churns, but I hold it in. "Maybe," I say.

After Ben is bathed and tucked into bed, I tell my mom I need to stay up to finish a school assignment. She sighs the sigh of someone who is perpetually tired. She can't exactly tell me not to do my schoolwork, but I know she wishes our apartment would be settled so she could go to bed in peace. Evan picks up on her mood.

"We could study at my house," he suggests. "I mean, would you be able to?"

My mom looks at me expectantly. Another door opening. Another step forward. Another give. Another take. She wants me to say yes. I don't want to let her down.

"Um, sure," I say.

Evan grins. My mom visibly decompresses.

"But not too late. And be quiet when you come home," she says.

I grab my school stuff and follow Evan out my front door and in through his. Even though I'm only going five steps from home, I'm jittery. My heart flutters fast and my palms sweat. There's that twist in my stomach that isn't quite nausea, but could be. There isn't a list taped to the wall to help me feel better if I need it. What if I need it? Because this is someone else's home. This is someone else's space. It's not where I spend my days or my moments of panic.

This is Evan's.

This is a place where I assume he lives a life that's full and rich and vibrant.

Evan flicks a switch by the front door and the living room lights up. His apartment is the flip-flopped version of mine, which only adds to the off-kilter feel of things. I look around and am surprised there are still moving boxes sitting in the middle of the floor.

"You haven't finished unpacking? It's been two months."

He laughs. "What? We've unloaded the basics."

I check out the boxes emblazoned with bold black letters: *COOKBOOKS, CHRISTMAS, ART SUPPLIES*. Hobbies and holidays packed into boxes and sealed shut.

"What can I say? We're not very organized. And my mom is crazy busy, as you know." He ticks his head toward the hallway. "This way. I gotta get my book."

He switches on the hall light. I follow him past his mom's fluttery skirts left to dry on hangers in the doorway of the bathroom and some paintings that haven't yet been hung. I stop to look at them and realize the paintings are portraits like mine. Connor's paintings. One of Evan. One of his mom. They're amazing.

Evan disappears into his room and turns on music while I stand staring. He switches on a song from last year that reminds me of swim practice because our coach would blast it from the speakers on the pool deck while we warmed up. It's a song I like. It's a song about good things.

Evan leans out of the doorway to look for me. "You lost?"

"Oh, I was just checking out the paintings. They're Connor's."

He nods.

"He really was good. I remember that." I turn away from Evan, studying the empty wall. "Do you want me to help you hang them?"

"Right now?"

"Well, yeah. I can help you get organized." I might be stalling. I've hung out in boys' rooms before, but it's been a long time.

"Morgan," Evan says in a way that makes me look right at him. "Don't be nervous. It's just a room. It doesn't have to be anything more than that. I promise."

Even though I spent the whole afternoon kissing Evan's mouth and pressing my thumbprint against the soft part of his neck between his earlobe and his jaw, I'm relieved to hear him say that his room is just a room. So I move my feet, one in front of the other, until I'm inside.

It's instantly clear that Evan's room is the most lived-in part of the apartment. He's taped posters to the walls of bands I've never heard of and daredevil surfers conquering monstrous waves. Under the window, there's a computer desk and a clunky-looking laptop with a Surfrider Foundation sticker stuck across the top of it. A mismatched desk chair, piled high with sweatshirts, is turned backward to face the room instead of the desk. The music switches to something lazy, and I turn to find where it's coming from. I spot his phone plugged into a dock propped on top of a bunch of surf magazines on the shelf underneath a small wooden nightstand. And next to that nightstand, in the middle of the room, is his queen-size bed. It's immaculately made, the pillows neatly lined up along the headboard.

"Yep. Just a room," I say.

Evan nods. His eyes don't falter.

I wander around the cramped space, leaning across his desk to get a closer look at a photograph he has tacked to the bottom corner of his bulletin board. It's one of those portraits people get done at the mall while wearing matching outfits. It's a family—a dad, a mom, and two kids, both boys.

"That's my dad," Evan says, leaning over my shoulder to point to the tall guy with dark Hawaiian skin. He looks like Evan with less fluffy hair. Evan draws circles around the mom and the kids with his index finger. "That's my dad's new family."

"Oh."

I understand then. And I think it might be an even worse rejection than what I feel from my own dad. Evan must feel like he's second best. I know my mom and Ben and I are second best to my dad's demons and addictions, but Evan is second best to two other kids. I wrap my arms around his waist, burying my face against his chest to hug him tight.

"I'm sorry," I mumble against his shirt.

"Thanks. I know you know." He sighs. Resigned. "We should study."

"In your room?"

"Is that cool? I like to play music when I'm working. And as you saw, the rest of the apartment isn't exactly user-friendly."

"Oh. Okay."

Evan sits down on the bed. I stand. I stare.

"Sorry." He leaps up and tosses the pile of sweatshirts from the desk chair to the floor. "Here."

I sit down and the chair sinks low, like one in a hair salon that needs to be pumped back up by the stylist. My knees are practically touching my chest, so I have to fumble with my notebook to spread it out across my lap. It's awkward and uncomfortable. Evan looks at me, stifling a laugh.

"I look ridiculous, don't I?"

"Not even. It's cute."

"It's okay." I stand up with my open notebook across my chest. "We can both sit on the bed."

Evan scoots over to make room for me, and I settle down next to him. I open my notebook and start highlighting sentences. He puts on a pair of reading glasses, settles against his pillow, and grips a copy of *1984* between his fingertips. The sight of him in those reading glasses just about does me in. I scoot in closer. He glances up from his book to look at me.

"Are we moving past the 'just a room' thing?" he asks.

"Kinda. Not completely. Still studying, just closer."

"Okay."

Evan looks down at his book again. I can't help watching him.

"So you wear reading glasses." A statement, not a question.

He rests his book on his chest. "Yeah, why?"

Because I love them? "No reason."

I stifle a hum of satisfaction as Evan tucks my head against his chest and goes back to reading, slowly raking his fingers through my hair. The feel of it makes goose bumps sprout up on my tailbone. He pulls a long strand of my hair apart from the others and wraps it around his thumb.

I try to concentrate on my notes, but they're all a big, giant blur. There's the music and his breathing and his heartbeat. And his reading glasses. I put my notebook down.

"Evan?"

"Yeah?"

"I need to ask you something."

He stops reading again and pulls my hair back, tucking it behind my ear. "Yeah?"

"Maybe you don't have a thing for Taylor, but are you sure she doesn't have a thing for you?"

He kisses the top of my head. "Never."

"So she's more like your BFF then."

Evan laughs, and his chest vibrates against my ear. "She's not my BFF. Do guys have BFFs?"

"Well, sure. Wasn't Connor your BFF?"

He thinks about that. "He was."

I fiddle with the edge of his shirt. "So Taylor could be your BFF. Guys and girls can be BFFs."

"But Taylor's not mine. I just met her at school. She wanted to learn to surf, and it was easy to teach her." He shrugs. "She told me all about how a bullet grazed her. She got lucky and she knows it. So now she's trying to be this total badass, but I have a feeling she used to have softer edges. Am I right?"

"Very. I don't even recognize the girl who showed up here today."

"I don't think she recognizes you, either." I recoil, and Evan feels it because he squeezes my shoulder to keep me with him.

"I'm not trying to be mean. I'm just saying the same thing I've always said: You're not the only one. You're not alone."

I nod, not sure what to say. I spend so much of my life telling Brenda about that day and how it affected me and how it made me who I am, but I haven't spent much time thinking about how it affected everyone else. It affected Taylor. It affected Evan. It affected Evan's aunt and his mom. It affected Chelsea, Brianna, and Sage, and a million other people. That's what Evan tried to tell me. I don't own the market on having sucky things happen to me. I've thought about all those other people, but in some ways, it was easier not to think about them too much. I'm certainly not the only one who lost something that day. Lots of people lost a lot more.

"Here's the thing," Evan says. "We're all just getting by, right? And sometimes it's easier to do that with someone who understands than to try to do it by ourselves."

"Oh, so you're some kind of savior or something?"

"I didn't say that. I'm not in the business of saving people. Truthfully? I think I'd suck at it. But I am in the business of surviving, so at least there's that."

He shifts his leg underneath me, and I fear my weight has become unbearable and cut off his circulation. Thankfully, it turns out he's simply moving to keep me where I am.

"So I have a question," he says through the soft light of the room. "And I want you to answer me honestly, okay?"

"Um, okay. You're scaring me. Is this like Truth or Dare?"

"Ha! You wish."

"No, you wish."

"Actually, I kinda do wish," he says, squeezing my shoulder with a laugh. "So okay, then, truth: Are you my girlfriend?"

That's so not what I was expecting and I go off-kilter a little. "I don't know, am I?"

"Do you want to be?"

"I have to admit I'm a little rusty."

He laughs. "That's okay. I can remind you how it works."

"Okay then."

"Yeah?"

I smile. "Yeah."

He shifts and I start to sink away from him until he grabs me and pulls me up onto his lap so I'm facing him, my legs draping over each of his thighs. My skirt hangs over our thighs like a blanket.

"I like it when you say that," he says, his hand squeezing my hip.

"Yeah?"

I inch my mouth closer to his. He nods.

"Yeah?" I ask again.

He nods a second time and kisses me.

The music is playing and we're lost enough in each other to drown out the world, which is probably why neither of us hears Evan's mom come home until she's banging around in the kitchen.

"Evan," she calls. "I'm home."

We pull apart. My cheeks heat. I try to pat down my hair as I scramble off his lap. Evan fumbles to tug his shirt back into place as he heads to the door of his bedroom.

"Wait. Where are you going?"

"To say hi to my mom." He looks at me like, *Duh*.

"But she'll know I'm in here."

"So?"

He opens the door just as his mom appears in the hallway. She looks surprised but not unhappy to see me hovering behind Evan in his bedroom.

"There you are. Hi." She smiles at me, then looks at Evan. "I just wanted to let you know I'm home. Can you turn down the music?"

"Sure." Evan opens the door to his room wider so I'm in full view. "Mom, you remember Morgan."

"Of course. It's so nice to see you again, Morgan."

"Thanks. You too," I say. "We're just doing homework."

My words come out really fast, making Evan do a double take. He grins at me. His mom claps her hands together like she just remembered something she has to do.

"Okay. Well. We've got a sink full of dishes, so I'm going to get to it." She heads back down the hallway and into the kitchen.

Evan turns to me, stifling a laugh. "Whoa."

"*Whoa?*" I narrow my eyes at him. "It's not funny." Evan might think his mom almost walking in on us is no big deal, but I don't. The panic is already happening. I can feel the hum of it in my head and in my bones. It's in my stomach and in my heart. I straighten

210

out my T-shirt and grab my notebook. "I need to go. Like, now." I shove everything into my bag and rush out his bedroom door.

"What? Why?"

"Your mom totally knows what we were just doing."

"So? She was seventeen once."

I try to picture Evan's mom at seventeen. Did she have the same long hair and triple-pierced ears? Did she know Evan's dad yet? Did she like school and football games?

Evan tries to pull me back, but I twist away from him and hurry down the hallway. My flip-flops flap furiously underneath my feet as I dash past the paintings that haven't been hung and the boxes that haven't been unpacked. Evan trails behind me, muttering something under his breath. I burst through the screen door and into the night. Outside, the air feels cool against my face, and I know it's because I'm flushed. Bright red. Mortified.

"Morgan, stop. It's okay."

The screen door slaps shut behind Evan. He stands still in bare feet, his board shorts slung low around his hips. A loose string from the hem of his thermal shirt trails down his thigh in a curlicue.

"Oh, my god. It's so not okay. That's the most embarrassing thing ever."

He pulls me toward him to kiss my forehead. "Don't worry. My mom's not weird about stuff like that."

"Evan, I was just straddling you on your bed. All moms are weird about stuff like that."

"Well, she doesn't *know* you were straddling me."

"Evan."

"What can I say?" He laughs. "My mom's weird about not being weird."

"I gotta go."

He hugs me and won't let go. And then his warm breath is in my ear, ticklish and tantalizing all at once. "Hey, I'm not embarrassed, okay?"

"I am."

"Don't be." He kisses me once. Gentle. Chaste.

"Yeah, right."

He leans back to look at me. His lips poke up into a teasing smile. He makes me want to smile, too.

"Stop it. Why do you always do that?"

"Do what?"

"Make me laugh."

He pushes back to lean against the balcony railing. The moon is a bright crescent high in the sky behind him. The breeze sways swiftly, picking up his fluffy curls in its wake. Like he's posing perfectly for a photograph.

"Morgan, don't you know? Making you laugh is my greatest accomplishment."

I roll my eyes, trying not to snort-laugh like Ben. "Don't be corny."

He shrugs. "Sometimes the truth is corny. Sometimes *I'm* corny. But you know that's why you like me." He smiles a smile that takes over his whole face, pressing his dimples deep into his cheeks. He pushes forward from the balcony railing and grabs for the handle of his screen door. He turns to me before he pulls it open. "Turn that phone back on, okay?"

"Okay."

I tiptoe through my apartment and down the hall. I do everything I can to keep the door to my room from creaking when I open it. I trip when I get halfway across the room because Ben has managed to kick off all his sheets so they're in a pile on the floor. My feet get tangled up in them as I grope through the dark to get to my bed. I slip off my skirt and pull my bra through the armhole of my T-shirt, then fall backward on top of my comforter, clutching Evan's old phone in my hand. It buzzes as soon as I turn it on.

Evan: *So actually not just a room.*

I have to stifle a giggle.

Me: *Smartass.*

Evan: *Smartass. Boyfriend. Whatever you want to call it, I'm happy. See you tomorrow.*

chapter thirty-five

"So I have a boyfriend," I tell Brenda as we stroll around the block, past dilapidated doorways and beaten-up bus stops two days later.

"Evan?"

"Yep."

I wait for her to say it's not okay. To say I'm not ready. Or I will ruin him. She takes a sip from her iced coffee, the sweaty condensation dripping down the sides of the cup and coating her fingertips, then looks at me thoughtfully.

"Morgan, I think that's positively wonderful."

"You do?"

She tweaks her neck in a double take. "Well, of course. Why wouldn't I?"

"Maybe because it was only last week that I set foot out of my front gate again?"

She sips. She sighs. "Getting out the front gate isn't the only thing that matters here. I know it might not always feel that way, especially with me, but it's true. Being open to new experiences and relationships is important, too."

I want to believe her. I want to trust her trust in me.

"Tell me about him," she says. "Evan."

It feels weird talking about this kind of stuff with Brenda. She's a grown-up. Right now, I miss Sage. I miss sitting at the lunch tables underneath the swaying palm trees while sharing play-by-plays of conversations and kisses.

"He makes me laugh. He doesn't sugarcoat things for me. He doesn't expect me to sugarcoat things for him. He doesn't tread lightly. He gets me."

I leave it at that because I can't tell her the other parts, like how it feels when Evan kisses me or itsy-bitsy-spiders his fingertips along my spine.

"It's a remarkable feeling, isn't it?" she says. "When someone gets you?"

I nod. A few feet ahead of us, a toddler becomes tangled up between his mom's legs. I push forward to catch his fall, but he rights himself just in time. Brenda doesn't notice. She's focused on me.

"I think Evan is good for you. And it sounds like you're good for Evan, too."

"Wow. Nobody has said anything like that to me in a long time."

"Like what?"

"That I was good for someone."

We stop. We stand.

"Morgan, of course you're good for people. What would Ben be without you? What would your mom be?"

I shrug. "I don't know. Unburdened?"

"Why do you think you're a burden?"

"Aren't I? It's all about me all the time."

"Is it?"

I think of our life. I think of my apartment and how it feels at the end of the day when everyone is home. I think of dinner and details. Of baths and bedtime stories. Of TV shows and talking. Of weekends and waffles. Of good nights and good mornings. Okay, so it's not all about me. It's about all of us.

"Fine. Maybe not all the time," I concede.

We head back to Paradise Manor. The sun is bright. School will be out for summer break in three weeks. We pass the corner market where Memorial Day decorations from the past weekend have easily morphed into Fourth of July decor. There are streamers and sparklers in a bin by the door. I want to buy a sparkler and light it up in the darkness of the night. I want to watch it sizzle and fizzle in my hand. It will pop and sputter, then disappear as if it had never caught fire in the first place.

Brenda tips her chin toward a trash can, crosses over, tosses her coffee cup, and turns back to me. "I can tell you you're not a burden. Your mom can tell you you're not a burden. But you have to believe it yourself. Will you try?"

"I always try."

"Yes, you do."

chapter thirty-six

There's no texting about whether Evan and I should hang out after school the next day; we just do. We sprawl out on chaise longues in the courtyard and move into my apartment when the other residents of Paradise Manor come home and open their windows wide enough to make the courtyard feel less private. We legitimately try to do homework because Evan really does need to raise his grade in trigonometry. But we keep getting distracted by each other. When he lifts his arms above his head to stretch, for instance, I can't help but notice the way his shirt rides up. And he looks so cute in his reading glasses. I think he might be wearing them on purpose now.

Today slips into tonight. We quit quizzing with notecards as the TV hums quietly in the background. Evan leans over to kiss me but pulls back when Ben races in, dumps his backpack on the floor, and stops still in front of me.

"Look out," he says, out of breath. "Mom's mad."

"Not good," Evan says as Ben races away from us. "I should go."

He stands up, but I pull him back down to the couch. "Stay. I'm sure it's fine."

My mom stomps through the house. She halts in front of me, waving an open envelope in one hand and a wrinkled piece of paper in the other.

"What is this? Really, Morgan! What is this?" she shouts.

She tosses both at me. They drift through the air, then land solidly on my lap. The envelope rests on my right thigh, writing side up.

My letter. My letter to Aaron Tiratore.

RETURN TO SENDER, ADDRESSEE UNKNOWN is stamped across the middle of it in bright red ink.

For three weeks, my letter has floated around in limbo with no idea where to go.

Evan looks at my lap. At the letter. At me. He tries to understand.

I pull up from the couch to close in on my mom. "You read it? You actually read my letter? How could you? That is such a violation!"

Evan is all ears. I'm all sweat and a quickened heartbeat. Also, a throbbing vein at my temple. My mom hasn't even acknowledged the fact that Evan's here. She couldn't care less that she's embarrassing me.

My mom points at me. "You do not owe that boy any kind of forgiveness, Morgan Grant. None. Zero."

I push up on the balls of my feet and lean in. "Wait. I don't or you don't?"

"Anyone! Nobody owes him a damn thing after what he did. And what are you even talking about here? What car ride? What does that mean?"

I glance at Evan. His face is angled down at his notebook. He works the tip of his pen through the metal spirals, releasing tiny flakes of paper onto his jiggling knee.

I look back at my mom. "Can we talk about this privately, please?"

"I'm gonna go," Evan says, bouncing up from the couch. He collects his things, but doesn't bother stuffing any of it into his backpack. He just leaves the room with papers and folders and half-open books hanging out from under his arms. Ben stands by the front door, shifting from one foot to the other like he has to pee.

"Come with me," Evan tells him, and they head out.

The door shuts with a rattle, and then it's just my mom and me and the murmur of the almost-muted voices on the TV.

"Well, that was pretty over-the-top. Did you have to do all of that in front of Evan?"

She doesn't hear me. She just launches into everything. "Why did you write this letter? Who did you hope would read it?"

"Nobody. The person I wrote it to is dead! You think I don't know that?"

She looks at me seriously, lowering her voice like she's going to tell me a secret. "Did you think his parents still lived there? Were you hoping they'd see it? Were you looking for answers?"

"God! I wasn't looking for anything, okay? It was just something I had to do. It was a relief. Like when I let go of it in the mailbox, I let go of other things, too."

Is that true? Is that all it was? Or did I hope, deep down, that Aaron's parents would see my letter and offer up some kind of an explanation? An apology? Something that would make me feel better? Because of course I knew they moved. Why would they stay? I'd even heard about the "For Sale" sign stuck into the crunchy brown grass of the front yard that people had defaced with red paint and rotten eggs. But if I knew they'd moved, then did I hope my letter would miraculously reach them? They had left without a trace. Nobody knew where they'd gone. And there's no way they would've left a forwarding address. They didn't want to be found. But I sent a letter anyway.

I sink back down onto the couch. I'm exhausted, as if I've just swum anchor for a relay race. My mom slumps down next to me. She pulls the letter from between the worn couch cushions. She holds it in her hand.

"His parents should've done better," she says. "They should've stopped him."

"Maybe they tried. All the news stories said he'd been in therapy. Maybe they couldn't do more than that," I say. "Maybe they tried everything until they had to stop caring."

"I guess that's how it might've been, huh?"

"Like with Dad."

My mom's back goes stiff. "Is that what you think? That I've stopped caring about your dad?"

I shrug. "I don't know." *Yes.*

My mom takes my hand and squeezes it. Her forehead crinkles. Her eyes get shiny. "Oh, Morgan. How can I say this in a way that you will understand? I care about your dad. But I care about you and Ben more. Does that make sense? That's why I don't understand Aaron's parents. How could they not have helped? He was their *son*. How could they not have known?"

"I know the choices you made for Ben and me. But parents

can't always know everything. Should you have known that I'd go crazy?"

"You're not crazy." She says it like I'm crazy for thinking I'm crazy.

"What about Dad? Is he crazy?"

She sighs. "Your dad is sick. Not crazy. I don't like that word, *crazy*."

Crazy does feel like it weighs a lot. It's a weight I've been grappling with ever since Aaron Tiratore stormed through the hallways of my school. What is *crazy*? Was Aaron crazy? Is it fair to call someone that?

"But you know Dad needs help," I say. "How are you any different from Aaron's parents if you don't get him help? The last time he was at Grandma's, it was like you didn't even want to try."

"Are you kidding? You know how hard I tried to get your dad help! But he's a grown man. I'm a mom, but I'm not *his* mom. I'm your mom. When you needed help, I got you help because that's what parents do. And when it was better for you and Ben to not have Dad around, I made that choice, too."

"Maybe it'd make you feel better to forgive him. Like I did with Aaron."

She looks at me, startled.

"That's why I wrote the letter," I say. "I had to forgive Aaron in order to forgive myself. Maybe you need to do the same thing."

"Maybe so." She leans back and stares up at the ceiling. The words feel so big, like they're just sitting there in a pile between us. Everything is quiet for a moment, and then my mom takes a deep breath like she's preparing herself. "What do you mean you need to forgive yourself? You didn't do anything wrong."

I answer her calmly. "I gave Aaron a ride to school on October fifteenth."

She pushes up, shaking her head like she didn't hear me right. "What?"

"Brenda knows. But I've been carrying it around. That guilt. I felt like it was partially my fault he did what he did because I drove him there."

"Oh, honey." She reaches for me. She has a look of pity on her face.

I hate that look.

"Please don't. I'm okay. I forgave myself. Because I forgave Aaron."

"I see."

We're quiet like that. There's the silence and the air and the light beaming down from the ceiling above us. When my mom stands up again, she shoves the letter back into the envelope and hands it over to me. I look at the RETURN TO SENDER stamp, blaring bright red and permanent. That stamp makes it seem like Aaron never existed. Like his life has been erased. He did what he did because he wanted people to remember him, but his name isn't even on the memorial wall.

chapter thirty-seven

After breakfast on Monday morning, I do aerobics in front of the TV with the windows open wide so the day can come in. I can do the whole workout now without running out of breath. I bounce from one foot to the other, pumping my fists up in the air while sweat drips down my face. After that, I put on my stretched-out Speedo and swim laps in the pool. I have no idea how far I go. The pool is only fifteen yards, so the laps are there and done too quick to count. Still, I can feel the strength in my muscles and my lungs and I have faint tan lines across my back again.

When I come back inside, wrapped in a towel, my hair dripping wet down my back, the home phone rings. The woman on the other end asks if either Carol or Morgan Grant is available, and I tell her that I am. She tells me her name is Karen and that she's calling from Pacific Palms Primary. Ben's school. My stomach flips up and over itself like a trapeze artist.

There's a scratchy sound followed by a bang, like she's muffling the phone with her hand. "I, um, I have a Mr. Richard Grant here to pick up Ben," she says. "He claims to be Ben's dad, but I don't have his name on the emergency release form. It says we can release Ben to you or Carol or his after-school program. Does Richard Grant have permission to take Ben?"

Everything stops long enough to feel like forever. And when the seconds start again, they're revved up like race cars.

"No. Don't let Ben go. He can't go with him." I say these things, panicked and petrified.

"He's, um, rather insistent," she says.

"I'm coming," I say. "I'm coming right now."

I turn off the phone and toss it onto the desk, then race down the hall to my room. I pull sweats on over my damp suit, run back through the apartment, and grab my car keys from the hook in the kitchen. Everything is automatic at first. Slapping through the screen door and tearing down the stairs and through the courtyard doesn't even faze me. But when I run out to the back of the building, I stop still at the line of marked parking spots. What I'm doing hits me full-force. I look at my car covered in the navy blue tarp. I can't move forward. I'm frozen, gripping my key ring in my hand. I grip it so tightly that the teeth of my house key dig into my palm enough to make an indentation.

And then I pace. I walk back and forth, from parking spaces 200 to 215. Counting up. Counting down. I can't do this. How can I do this? I sink to my knees, trying to catch my breath. My stomach churns. I lurch forward like a cat. I retch. Nothing comes up. I pant in place until the warm pavement soaks through the knees of my sweatpants and scrapes the palms of my hands. What good am I?

And then I think of Ben. I think of the googly eyes on his frog costume and the way he pronounces the word *paleontologist* incorrectly when he talks about dinosaurs. I think of the way he squeezes my cheeks between his hands so I can't say "I love you" coherently before he kisses me. I think of the way he sleeps and runs and jumps and dreams. I think of all that he doesn't know and all that he shouldn't have to know. Not yet. And because of that, I stand up and yank the tarp off my car, leaving it in a crumpled mess on the ground.

I get inside and shove the key into the ignition. The engine growls in protest from so many months of not being driven while the exhaust pipe coughs up black smoke into the alley.

I sit for a moment.

My seat rumbles underneath me.

I grip the steering wheel.

I look over my shoulder.

I back my car out.

I go.

When I round the corner and merge into traffic, there are lights and bikes and people and things that make me jerk in my seat. I continually start and stop my car with a jolt, trying to avoid everyone and everything. Even though I'm alone, all I can see is Aaron Tiratore sitting next to me clutching a backpack full of secrets. I dry-heave at a stoplight and quickly roll down all the windows in case I puke for real.

He's not here. He only exists if I let him.

It's just before ten a.m. when I peel into the lower lot of Ben's school. I don't even check to make sure I'm parked between the lines. It seems like it should be time for recess, like kids should be hanging upside down from monkey bars or slurping up tubes of yogurt and juice boxes. But the campus is quiet and empty, and I worry that it's because of my dad. Especially since there's also a police car parked in front of the school. I know it's bad. Not Aaron Tiratore bad, but still bad.

I run up the concrete steps, past the handmade posters advertising Ben's play four days from now, and through the front door of the office. I must be loud, because everyone turns to look at me at once—two police officers, one principal, one secretary, and both of my parents.

I zero in until my mom and dad are all I see.

My mom is frazzled and furious, her eyebrows and fists knitted tight as she shifts from foot to foot. My dad is slumped over and slender in a chair by the window, his wrists handcuffed behind his back. I haven't seen him in over a year and a half, but the way he looks now is beyond anything I expected. He's gaunt. He's dirty. He has a ratty beard with food crumbs stuck in it. I can smell the stench of alcohol and filth on him from ten feet away. Seeing him makes my heart hurt for so many reasons.

My mom turns to me, her eyes filling up with tears. "You came."

I well up. I can't help it. Her words mean everything.

"Where is he? Is he okay?" My eyes are everywhere, but I don't see my brother, and all I can think is that something happened to him.

"He's in class," my mom says. "He doesn't even know."

"I don't understand," I say. "Why are the police here?"

"Because your dad wouldn't take no for an answer."

"I just want to see my son," my dad says. It seems like a simple enough request from a father, but nobody in his right mind would consider sending a kid off with someone who looks like my dad right now.

"You want to see Ben?" I ask him. My words are loud. "You actually want to see him? Since when have you had any interest in seeing any of us?" The noise of my voice carries through the tiny office, over the desk and through the slats of the ceiling fan, making the principal and my mom jump. "Christmas, birthdays, swim meets, awards ceremonies . . ." I tick them off until my voice quiets to a whisper. "And when all those kids at my school died, I could've died, too. But you come now. Why now?"

"Because he's my son. I needed to see him."

He only wants to see Ben. He doesn't want to see me. As much as I lectured my mom about forgiving my dad, the truth of him not wanting to see me hurts. "He doesn't even know you," I say. "I'm the one who knows you."

Those words make my dad's shoulders tense. My mom gapes at me. Maybe I've only focused on forgiving Aaron Tiratore. Because right here, right now, I don't feel like I've forgiven my dad.

"What? It's true."

My mom nods slightly. She knows I'm right. "Morgan," she says, "maybe it would be better for you to wait outside." She looks pointedly at my dad. "She's been through a lot. And your absence hasn't helped."

"Oh, yeah. Here we go again. I'm always the bad guy," my dad says.

"Are you for real?" My mom tosses her purse to the floor, like she had to throw something, but that's all she had. "You're actually

227

going to play the victim here?" She angles her body in front of him. "You know what? Your daughter, *our* daughter, who I've come to realize is smarter than you and me put together, thinks I should forgive you. She thinks forgiving you will help us move on. She's a better person because she's been able to forgive people who have done unforgivable things. I wish I were capable of such forgiveness, but I'm not. Because I will never, in a million years, forgive this." She sweeps her hands in front of my dad in a gesture of disgust. "Showing up this way, making a scene at your son's school? It's unforgivable. Absolutely, positively unforgivable. You need help. I will never allow you to see Ben until you get it."

"Or me," I say. "Not that you seem to care about that."

My dad lifts his head to look at me, and when he does it's like I'm only a memory of something from a long time ago. It's true that I know him and Ben doesn't. But that's the problem. That's exactly why he doesn't want to see me. I'm a reminder of him at his best. And that makes what he is now even worse. Of course he'd rather spend time with a trusting six-year-old who doesn't entirely understand how messed up his dad is. I'm not like that. My dad knows I know how much he has changed. He slumps over in his chair. The hem of his jacket, dirt-stained and tattered, drapes past his knees, skimming the floor. His arms stretch behind him, the handcuffs biting into his wrists, as he erupts into huge, heaving sobs. He looks so weak. I don't even know who he is as he shakes and sniffs in front of me. I don't recognize a single thing about him.

And then my mom cries, too, and I'm wondering if she wants to take back her words.

Behind the desk, the principal straightens out her smart pink sweater set and the secretary stares off at her computer screen, presumably trying not to invade what feels like a private family moment.

"Let's go," the taller police officer finally says, pulling my dad up by the elbow.

"Wait!" My mom stops them at the door, gently reaching for my dad's shoulder because she knows her touch might startle him. "Rich," she says. "Please let them take you someplace where you can get help."

He looks down at her, eye to eye, searching for something. But his face switches to confused. Disoriented. Like he doesn't remember who she is or how he got here.

My mom and I follow the police and my dad out. The school bell rings and kids instantly spill out of classrooms, babbling loudly and swinging lunch boxes in their hands. I don't know why they're out here. I thought they were keeping everyone inside. I must've just had an idea in my head that the stillness of the campus meant the administration and the teachers were keeping our secrets. But they weren't. And now, I look up and there's Ben standing in front of us, watching the stairs. He shifts. He squints. His superhero lunch box dangles at his side.

"Morgan," he sputters, "is that Dad?"

chapter thirty-eight

My mom calls into work to say she has a family emergency and can't return. Then she checks Ben out of school for the day. There's no point in staying. She has to tell him things he might not be ready to hear but that need to be explained nonetheless. Because today my dad went too far. And now my mom has to tell Ben how sick his dad is and that he needs to get help from special doctors to get better. She has to tell Ben that no matter what, he should never go anywhere with our dad. I assume we'll go straight home to talk then stare at the walls and each other, but Ben begs for ice-cream cones like an unexpected afternoon off from school equals an insta-vacation.

"Think you can handle ice cream?" my mom asks me while Ben jumps up and down, pleading for me to say yes.

I don't know if I can handle it or not. The only way to know for sure is to go. That is what Brenda has taught me. That's what I've been doing every day. Attempting and accomplishing things bit by bit.

"I want to try," I say.

My mom squeezes my hand. "We'll be right there with you."

She and Ben follow me home to drop off the Bel Air. Knowing they're right behind me makes the drive back way less stressful than the drive to Ben's school. We ditch my car and pile into hers, where I sit in the back with Ben. His shoulders are even with mine thanks to the added height from his car seat. But not driving makes me feel even more trapped. I can feel the sweat collecting along my hairline and the barfy grumblings of my stomach.

"Windows," I yelp, and my mom presses a button to roll down all four of them at once.

The wind blows in my face. It's enough to keep the nausea at bay, but I'm totally counting the blocks down as we go. Three more. Two more. One more. I haven't seen this part of town in so long, but I know it as well as I know all of Ben's lines in his play. I miss it. I miss being here. And I'm so relieved when we pull into a parking space and I plant my feet on the solid sidewalk again. Ben leads us to the shack at the end of the pier like he's on auto-pilot. We get soft serve ice cream and not enough napkins—a huge mistake since the remnants of Ben's chocolate cone get smeared across his face like war paint.

We sit at the end of the pier and watch the ocean and the boats and every significant movement in our world at that moment. Tons of people are out even though it's the middle of the day. There's a false notion that people who live by the beach have money, but the reality is that burnt-out surf bums and dozing homeless people are also scattered among the moms dressed in designer sweatpants and thirtysomething entrepreneurs who make their own hours.

Ben scrunches his face up as he watches a homeless guy shuffling from person to person on the pier, holding his stained pants up with one hand and asking for spare change with the other.

"Does my dad do that?" Ben asks.

"Probably, sometimes," my mom says.

"Why?"

And there's the question we can't completely answer. Still, my mom tries.

"Because he needs help. Not just with money to buy food, but with a lot of other things, too. But he needs to figure out for himself that he needs help. Grandma and I can tell him, but he has to want to get it."

"So when he gets help, he'll come back?" Ben asks.

"It might not be that simple," I say.

"But what if I want him to get help so I can still love him?"

"It's okay to love him no matter what," my mom says. "And it's okay if you miss him and want him to get better, because Morgan and I want that, too."

Ben bites into the cone of his soft serve and chews thoughtfully. "Okay. That's what I'll do then."

After eating, we head back. My mom swings Ben's hand in hers, the wind whipping her bun loose so the shiny brown strands of her hair brush her shoulders. It's just the three of us—the way it used to be when we'd spend warm evenings or sunny weekend mornings here like this. We make our way up the pier where we pass fishermen and moms pushing babbling toddlers in baby strollers. We pass runners wearing formfitting Lycra tank tops and neon shoes. We pass a girl who looks a little older than me hustling to the ice-cream shack, tying her bright pink apron around her waist while balancing her phone between her ear and her shoulder.

And I have a memory then. Of days at the beach with my dad when I was just a little kid and it was only the two of us with a boogie board and a bottle of sunblock. He taught me how to swim in the ocean, navigate waves, and get out of rip currents. Ben wants my dad to get help so he can still love him while I've tried to pretend I don't love my dad because of who he's become. I don't love this new version of him. I miss the old one. But that's not the whole truth. Because my dad is going to be my dad forever. He's going to be my dad whether he gets help or doesn't. The truth is I will love him either way because he's my dad. I will love what I remember. But loving isn't the same as forgiving, and I still need to work on that.

About halfway up the pier, Ben stops at a binocular stand that costs twenty-five cents. My mom fishes out her wallet to come up with a quarter for him. We sit down on the bench next to the stand to stare out at the horizon while Ben looks through the binoculars at some stand-up paddleboarders way off in the distance. It's weird to say, but I already miss this moment. I'm longing for something before it's even gone. It makes me want to do everything I can to keep having moments like this.

My mom's phone rings as we're heading back to the car. She answers. "It's the police," she tells me, and ducks behind a concrete column to talk.

I pull Ben to the wide front window of a nearby bakery, where we watch a man in a hairnet roll out dough across the floured surface of a butcher-block table. He has a bunch of metal cookie cutters laid out next to him, and I ask Ben if he can tell what shapes they are. He squints and takes inventory.

I look over at my mom. She's fidgety, nodding her head, and clipping and unclipping the clasp on her purse.

Ben looks up at me, ticking off all the shapes, and I nod with enthusiasm. "Good job," I say. "I think you figured out all of them."

My mom is only on the phone for a few minutes, and she looks shell-shocked when she walks back over to us.

"What is it? What happened?" I ask.

"I don't believe it. Your dad willingly checked into rehab. He actually did it." Her eyes tear up, but they're tears of relief. Of happiness. Of hope.

I have them, too.

Just a few minutes ago we were on the pier, escaping reality. Now reality is back. But it's a good reality. It's a promising one.

chapter thirty-nine

Evan insists that going to Ben's play is our first date. So on Friday night, we drive in his car to make it more official. His music is good. The windows are down. The air is salty. I want to love the moment more than I do.

But I can't.

Because the reality is that I'm about to do the thing I've been worried about ever since Ben told me he was in a play. I'm about to sit down with a bunch of strangers and pretend like it doesn't bother me.

"Pull over," I say only three blocks past Paradise Manor.

I scramble out of the car and sit down on the curb. I take deep breaths while the evening traffic rush comes and goes through several cycles of red, yellow, and green traffic lights in front of us. East and west. North and south. Evan sits, too, quietly watching the cars with me. He doesn't talk. He doesn't tell me to get over it. He just lets me work through my moment. I appreciate that.

It's why I get back in the car.

He holds my hand for the rest of the drive, squeezing it every once in a while to remind me I've got this. And then he holds my hand through the lobby, past the door, and down the aisle of the auditorium. He finds me an end seat in case I need to make a quick escape, then sits down to the left of me. He tosses his jacket on the seat next to him to save it for my mom, who had to come earlier to help Ben get ready backstage.

And then we sit. And wait. And watch.

I visualized every single second of this with Brenda, but it's still different when I'm actually living it.

Everyone except us has some form of recording device. Before anything has even started, parents are taping the audience filing in or snapping pictures of themselves holding up the program. I try to record a memory of the scene. I snap a visual of the chocolate-brown velvet curtain skirting the sides of the stage. It's open wide enough to see the cute kid-painted forest scene that will be used as the backdrop for the play. There are white fluffy clouds and trees hanging low and dotted with lush green leaves and bluebirds. The sounds of flowing river water and forest animals echo through the sound system.

As we sit, the auditorium gets more packed with people. Lightweight jackets are shed and hung over the backs of seats, and cell phones are whipped out for last-minute checks of e-mail and other pressing things. I take inventory of every face and emergency exit.

"It's nice to be out with you," Evan says, squeezing my hand and distracting my brain. "In the world, I mean."

I squeeze back. "Thanks for bringing me."

"Come on, you know there's nobody else I'd rather spend opening night of Pacific Primary's kindergarten musical with than you."

I lean over to kiss him discreetly on the cheek. My kiss is innocent enough that someone might just think we're friends who haven't seen each other for a while. But then Evan pulls me closer and presses his mouth to mine with a little more passion. I squelch a laugh.

"We're at a play being put on by six-year-olds. Stop."

"Okay. Sorry." He pulls my hand back to his lips and kisses each of my knuckles. One, two, three, four, five.

I recognize the principal when she walks down the aisle and up the steps at the side of the stage to stand in front of the microphone to thank us for coming. She's wearing a sweater set similar to the one she wore on the day my dad showed up at Ben's school. I wonder if she owns anything other than sweater sets. I try to picture her at the beach, and it's impossible to imagine her in a bathing suit or eating ice cream or diving through a wave. Tonight's cardigan has some gold zing on it, so it must be extra dressy for school plays or something. I only notice the zing because the spotlight is on her and it's making the gold spray sparkles across the auditorium.

She talks about the play and how impressive it is that kindergartners memorized all these lines and songs. She thanks Ben's teacher and the parents who helped make costumes and are selling cookies in the lobby. She talks about a fund-raiser and a box tops contest. Everyone applauds because they're supposed to.

My mom scoots past my legs to take her seat. "Ben is so nervous. I hope he doesn't barf onstage," she says.

"I hope I don't barf right here."

She squeezes my shoulder, then sits down on the other side of Evan.

The curtain closes and the lights dim until the curtain re-opens. And then the overhead lights tint the stage with green and gold to make it look like a forest flecked with sunlight. Out comes Ben, alone, hop, hop, hopping. He's so cute that it makes everyone in the audience titter with laughter. The green hood of his sweatshirt hangs low over his face, and his googly eyes roll all over the place.

"One, two, three, four! Come explore the forest floor," Ben calls, and a few more kids dressed as various forest animals skitter onto the stage.

My grin is as wide as our row of seats. I could watch this forever.

Until, behind me, there's the sound of heavy footsteps. There's a whispered "Excuse me" as a guy who looks close to my age settles into a seat across the aisle from me. He's wearing a heavy coat even though it's kind of hot in here, and he's carrying a backpack even though it's way past school hours. I'm almost positive I hear a metal clanging sound coming from his bag as he slowly slides it between his legs, settling it gently on the floor between his feet. It's all a little too familiar. The rational part of me knows he's doing things this way to be polite. To be quiet. To not interrupt the frog and the squirrel talking on the stage. But the part of me that gave Aaron Tiratore a ride to school bolts up from my chair, heart pounding and stomach churning, to race up the aisle of the auditorium. I know I'm loud and clunky because everyone in the audience turns to look at me as I go. I crash through the door to the lobby with a boom. The last thing I see before the door shuts behind me is Ben.

And I want to yell, *Stop! Get off the stage!*

But I can't move. I can't make a scene. Because it's fine. It's probably fine.

What if it's not fine?

I walk back through the door, down the aisle, and right up to the boy and his backpack. I tap him on the shoulder and attempt to grab his bag at the same time.

"I need to check this," I say louder than I should, like I'm important enough to have that right. He tries to pull it away from me.

"Morgan! Sit down!" my mom hisses.

Evan looks back and forth from me to the guy like he's trying to figure out what's going on. Really, everyone is looking at me. And I know what they're thinking. *Who is this crazy girl with the nerve to cause such a disruption at an adorable kindergarten play?* Why don't they realize I might be saving all of them?

It gets even worse when the kindergarten forest animals stop in the middle of their performance to watch. I can see Ben squinting at me through the rainbow-colored stage lights. And I know it's time to take my meltdown right on out of this auditorium. I give the backpack one final tug until I have it, and when I start walking back up the aisle with it, the guy has no other choice but to follow me.

"What're you doing? Who are you?" he asks, trying to pull

his bag from me when we reach the lobby. I yank it back and unzip it.

"I just need to check this," I say.

When I look inside, I see two binders, a book, and an aluminum water bottle—that must be what made the clanging sound—staring back at me. I unzip the smaller pocket in front to dig around through pens, pencils, and pennies. And I know how crazy I really seem. Once I'm satisfied, I hand his backpack over to him.

"Thanks," I say. "All good."

"Seriously? You're weird," he grumbles, zipping the backpack up. "If my sister's scene wasn't coming up, I'd report you to security or something."

And then he's gone. And I'm left standing here in front of a bunch of sweet-looking moms acting like they're too busy loading plastic plates with cookies and cupcakes for intermission to pay attention to what just happened. Except for one of them. One of them watches me, frozen, with a fluffy pink cupcake in her hand. When Evan shows up, I pull past him and through the front doors of the auditorium into the cool air and dusky twilight. I leave the warm lights of the theater lobby behind me and run to find a place to hide. I finally settle on the wall around the corner. I slide down it. It's smooth, like marble, so it doesn't hurt my back or catch my shirt. I sit on my butt, holding my thighs tight to my chest. I rest my forehead against my knees and try to breathe.

"Morgan?" Evan whispers from around the corner, as if we're still inside and he doesn't want to interrupt the performance.

I rock back and forth, back and forth.

"Morgan," he tries again.

"I'm over here," I say. "Lurking in the shadows. Like a vampire."

He chuckles as he rounds the corner and slides down next to me. He knocks his knee against mine. "You okay? Was it too dark, maybe?"

"I don't think my problem was the lights being out."

"I meant the play. That was some pretty dark shit for a bunch of kindergartners. All those forest animals trying to find their way across the river before dinnertime? Mind blown." He unfolds his fingers on each side of his head to indicate explosions.

I smile at him through the evening light.

"I freaked out when I saw the backpack," I say.

"I know." I like that he knows. I like that I don't have to explain more than that.

We sit quietly for many minutes, just breathing in the salty smell of the summer air while Evan traces circles in the palm of my hand with his fingertip. Around and around he goes until at least ten minutes pass, which feels like a lot when your brother is the star of the play.

"I made a scene." I sigh.

"Honestly, I don't think anyone really even understood what was going on. The play's just that good." I actually giggle. "It's okay. We'll just sit here until you're ready to go back in."

"Ben saw me leave. He knows I'm gone."

"Then don't be gone."

"I've missed so much already."

"Don't miss any more."

He stands up.

He reaches for my hand.

I take it.

chapter forty

"I freaked out at Ben's play," I tell Brenda the next Tuesday as I sip a Slurpee on the hood of my car in a 7-Eleven parking lot a few blocks from my house. Brenda has an iced coffee, which I've come to realize is her drink of choice. It's the last week of school for Evan, Ben, and me. I have final projects and an appointment with a testing proctor to freak out over, but instead of working on them, I'm spending the afternoon doing driving lessons with Brenda. They're nothing like the lessons I took with my high school's PE teacher when I was fifteen and got my learner's permit. Instead, Brenda's teaching me tricks to what she's dubbed "maintaining the brain" in my car.

"I missed practically the whole first half of the performance," I say, remembering how disappointed Ben looked when I hugged him into my arms in the lobby. "He asked me where I went during 'the best scene of the whole thing.' I felt awful."

"What did you say?"

"I told him a half truth. I said I didn't feel good and needed some air. And that I went back as soon as I could."

Brenda takes a long look at me. "That's fair."

"Is it? He's just a little kid, and I totally let him down."

"You did the best you knew how to do at the time. It's not uncommon to have setbacks, Morgan. That's okay as long as you don't let those moments define you. You went back inside and saw the rest of the play. That's what matters."

"I guess so."

Brenda lifts her dreadlocks away from her neck. She uses them like a fan to air herself out in the heat of the day.

"It's hot," I acknowledge.

"It is. Do you mind if I run in and grab a refill?" She shakes her empty cup at me, and the melting ice cubes bounce against the plastic.

I hesitate a little. The idea of sitting here alone with my thoughts is unsettling. But it's not like Brenda's running across town. She's going fifty feet away. I can watch her the whole time.

"Okay, yeah," I say, like I'm talking myself into it. "Go ahead."

"I'll be quick." She slides off the hood of my car, being careful not to scratch it. "Need anything else?"

I shake my head, holding up my Slurpee. "I can't even finish this."

I dig my fingernails into the palm of my hand as I watch Brenda head inside and toward the self-serve aisle. But I turn from watching her when a group of buff construction workers pull up in two separate trucks on either side of my car. They hop out, dirty work boots hitting the asphalt, and pat their pants pockets in search of cigarettes. One of them looks at me, his long dusty hair floating over his eyelids. He's tall and lanky, not like the other ones. He still looks like a teenager. He nods hey, like he knows me.

He doesn't.

"Nice ride," he says, motioning to my car. His Southern accent tells me he didn't grow up in Pacific Palms.

When I don't respond, he smirks.

"Oh, I see how it is. Too good for me, eh?" He shakes his head, moving closer. "You local girls kill me."

I do a quick take over my shoulder, feeling the need to plan an escape route. When he leans against the driver's side door to help himself to a peek inside my car, my heart hiccups and my insides ripple. I look through the window of the 7-Eleven for Brenda, willing her to hurry up and get out here. She's in the checkout line, watching us. She gives me a warm smile, like this creepy dude is no big deal.

"Clean dash. How old?" the guy says, swiping his index finger across the top of my steering wheel.

I dig my nails deeper into the palm of my hand. "It's a fifty-seven."

"Wow. Someone must really like you." He looks me up and down in a way that lets me know he means the double entendre.

I need Brenda to get out here right now. What's taking her so long? I glance back inside to see her laughing at something the store clerk is saying. The guy leans against the driver's side door and rests his elbow on the roof of the Bel Air.

"Please don't touch my car," I say. The words come out sounding more like a plea than a demand.

He takes a couple steps back, slowly looks me up and down

again, and puts his hands up in surrender. "Chill out, Local Girl. I'm just looking." He shakes his head and saunters toward the door of the 7-Eleven. He hits the entrance at the same time Brenda is exiting, and I watch him as he moves aside to hold the door open for her. She thanks him and walks toward me with a smile on her face, like she's still enjoying whatever it was the clerk said to her in there.

"Way to take your time," I say, carefully sliding off the car, ready to leave.

She grabs my elbow to stop me. "Hey now, what are you so upset about?"

"Didn't you see me getting harassed out here by Mr. Psycho?"

"Mr. Psycho? You mean the cute guy who was standing by your car? What did he do? Did I miss something?"

I notice he's watching us through the window. He's ripped open a bag of potato chips and is eating them right there in the middle of the store before he's even paid for them. He looks more curious than anything, like I've just baffled him somehow.

"That guy was practically climbing into my car and you didn't even notice! You were too busy making friends with everyone inside the 7-Eleven!"

Brenda jerks back from my words just as a mom with two kids comes out the door. She stops to look at us. I guess I'm going to be loud right here in the middle of the parking lot in the middle of the day.

"You brought me outside and abandoned me!"

"That was not abandonment, Morgan. And I didn't come running out to your rescue because I didn't see anything that looked worrisome."

"Well, maybe that shows how little you know."

"Oh, really? And you know everything, do you?" Brenda slams her drink down on the roof of my car, making me flinch. She better not have made a scratch.

"I know that guy was creepy. I know that much."

"Fine. Talk to me. What about him made you nervous?"

"Everything!"

"I want you to be specific. Did he remind you of Aaron?"

"No."

"Did he say something that troubled you?"

"He was definitely overly friendly."

"And that made you uncomfortable."

"Yes. And if you really cared, you would've recognized it. But I guess you don't care. I guess I'm nothing but a professional duty to you."

"Are you kidding? You are so much more than a professional duty to me. You *are* me!" She stops herself, shaking her head, realizing what she said.

"What does that mean?"

"Nothing. I'm sorry. I shouldn't have said that. Let's go."

She grabs her coffee and walks around to the passenger side of my car. I don't exactly want to spend time with Brenda in a confined space right now, but when the construction workers head back out to their trucks, I scramble into the driver's seat. The guy who was all over my car gives me a sarcastic military hand salute as he passes me.

"You're right. He's kind of creepy," Brenda mutters.

I turn to look at her. "I told you."

She shrugs her shoulders, but she still seems peeved because she doesn't look at me.

"Oh, now you're annoyed with me?"

"I'm not annoyed, Morgan. You can just be extra challenging sometimes. That's all."

I turn to face her. "If I'm so challenging, why do you even bother?"

"Because I'm up for the challenge, dammit!" But just as Brenda always manages to do when she loses it, she instantly mellows out, like an automatic calm-down checklist clicks into place in her head. I guess she has better control over her emotions than I do. When she's caught up with herself, she lets out a heavy sigh and finally meets my eyes again. "I think it might be useful for me to disclose something about myself. I'd like to explain why I wanted to help you, and this seems like as good a moment as any. Would that be okay?"

I focus on the tattooed vines weaving up her arm and under the sleeve of her shirt, poking back out again from her neckline. "Yes. I'd like that."

"We have a similar background, you and me. I grew up in an apartment like yours with a family like yours. My dad was in the military. I was in high school when he came back from Iraq. He was not in good shape. He completely checked out from our family."

"I know the feeling."

"I know you do."

"Did he get better?"

"No. He killed himself."

"Oh, god."

She looks at me then gently presses her fingers to my wrist. "I'm not saying that is the end result for everybody, Morgan. It most definitely is not. Please don't worry about this with your own father. You can find comfort in knowing he has chosen to get help." She sighs. "I wish my dad had done the same. Because what he did hurt me deeply. I blamed myself somehow, thinking I should've known he would do it. Thinking I should've been able to stop him. The guilt haunted me. I wanted to talk to someone. I asked my mom if we could look into therapy. It took a lot for me to ask for that kind of help. I was embarrassed. None of my friends had therapists that I knew of. And my mom acted like I should just find a way to get through it." Brenda looks at me, truthful and trusting. "It was like she didn't hear me."

"So you never talked to anyone?"

"Not until I was older. In college. It essentially led me to my career." She smiles at me. "Morgan, when you came to my office and you were so honest with your mom about your fears and why you couldn't go to school, it felt like you didn't think you were being heard." She squeezes my forearm. "I wanted you to know I heard you."

"Thank you," I say, my voice catching.

"You're welcome."

I pick at the edge of the steering wheel. "I'm sorry I said what I said before."

"It happens."

"You're actually really brave."

"So are you."

After a few minutes of sitting there, only breathing, Brenda buckles her seat belt.

"Ready?" she says.

I nod and buckle in. I start the engine and back out. We drive along a curved road by the beach. The sand and the ocean are spread out in front of us. I take it all in, I try to enjoy it, as we drive back to Paradise Manor.

I park my car in space 207 out back, and Brenda stands underneath the shade of the overhang as I pull the tarp back over the Bel Air.

"I'd really like it if we could meet at my office from now on," Brenda says, sounding very matter-of-fact. "And I think we can cut our meetings down to just one time per week. Drop Thursdays, keep Tuesdays. You're ready."

"How do you know? I just freaked out in the 7-Eleven parking lot. I don't think I'm ready."

She looks at me. "Morgan, you're ready."

"But I need you. I can't do this without you." I wave my arms around, trying to communicate that the world is still too big and overwhelming.

"You won't be doing it without me. I'll still work with you in my office. And I'm only a phone call away if you need me some other time."

I feel a panic attack coming on. I'm pretty sure Brenda is not supposed to make me feel this way.

"I can't do it."

"Morgan," Brenda says, "you're already doing it."

chapter forty-one

That afternoon, after Brenda and I have finished my driving lesson and I've made a nausea-inducing phone call to my testing proctor to confirm that I'll be at my final exams at the Ocean High library tomorrow, Evan shows up at my door. He hands me a disc as he crosses the threshold. I turn over the clear plastic case in my hand. It doesn't have a label.

"What's this? Another surf video?"

"Nope. It's Ben's play."

I look at him. "What? How?"

Evan shrugs. "I made friends with some parents with a camera while you and your mom were hugging all over Ben in the lobby after the show. They burned me a copy, and I picked it up today."

I kiss him. "You're amazing. Have I told you that?"

"Not in so many words."

We settle on the couch, the DVD player whirring to a start. Evan reaches over to scoop my legs across his lap.

"So, last day of school tomorrow for both of us," he says, walking his fingertips across my bare knee.

"Don't remind me. I have to take three on-site finals tomorrow. I'm not looking forward to it."

"Where?"

"Your school."

"So I'll wait for you. Out in the hall."

"You would do that?"

"Sure. If it'll make you feel better knowing I'm there."

"I would like that. So much."

"Then it's done. I'll be there. And just think: when you finish, it'll be summer. Officially. Am I gonna be able to get you down to the beach and on a surfboard in the next two months?"

"I hope so." And I mean it.

"Good. I can't wait." He flashes the remote at the TV. "Ready to watch Ben?"

"Definitely."

Evan presses play, and the DVD starts with a couple jerky movements but steadies itself quickly. And then there's Ben hopping across the stage. He's so cute, I can't stand it. I actually tear up watching him. The DVD is about an hour long, and it's bittersweet to see the twenty minutes I missed, especially the part where a kid sings half of a peppy song with his back accidentally turned to the audience. By the end of it, I'm bawling. I promise Evan they're happy tears. Ben steals the show, and I'm pretty sure I'm not saying that because I'm biased. He could probably earn big money being one of those annoying kid actors.

"I wish I'd seen the whole thing for real." I sigh, leaning back into the couch cushions. "That was the best."

"So you'll go to the next one. And the one after that. I'm pretty sure that's not gonna be Ben's last starring role."

I laugh. "I think you're right."

We sit in silence for a minute, watching the dark screen of the television until Evan grabs the remote and switches the TV back to the regular stations. My stomach clenches, because the news is on. They're at Pacific Palms High School. They're standing in the courtyard. In front of the memorial wall. There are lots of flowers. And solemn faces. My former PPHS principal is behind a podium saying important things. Evan aims the remote at the screen to change the channel, but I hold his wrist steady.

"Don't," I say. "We should watch."

"Are you sure?"

I nod. So we do. We watch. And then I see Evan's mom. She's holding the hand of a woman who looks just like her. On the other side of her, holding the woman's other hand, is Evan. And of course they're there. PPHS will reopen in the fall, and they dedicated the official memorial wall today. And Evan's cousin's name is on the wall. Connor Wallace. They must've filmed this earlier. After morning finals and before he picked up the DVD of Ben's play and brought it here.

"My aunt," he mumbles. "She needed us."

"That must've been so hard." I squeeze his hand. "I'm sure you miss him a lot."

"Every day." He stares at the screen. At his mom. At his aunt. At himself. "He was one of my favorite people. He was an only child and I was an only child, so early on, we decided we'd be like brothers."

I pull my legs from Evan's lap so I can wrap my arms around him. I squeeze him tight. "I'm sorry I haven't asked about Connor. I should have. But I wasn't sure if I could handle talking about it, which is so selfish and wrong."

"I understand."

"It's hard to miss someone."

The muscle in his jaw ticks. "It sucks to miss someone."

"Did you see him a lot? Even living so far apart?"

"Every summer and every spring break. It's not exactly hard to get people to visit when you live in Hawaii. We grew up surfing together, so that's pretty much all we did when we saw each other." Evan smiles thoughtfully. "But he threw lemons at rental cars, too. You know, just to fit in." He pinches my elbow.

"So you were totally BFFs!"

He laughs. "Yep. Pretty much."

"Evan, I'm so sorry." I hug him again. "I really am."

When I pull back, he sits there looking at me so gently with his big brown eyes. There's a rip at the hem of his T-shirt and another one on the knee of his jeans. There's stubble on his chin and a pimple on his forehead. There's a scar on his right arm where he told me he got nailed by the skeg of his surfboard when he was in middle school. He isn't perfect. There's the pain of loss underneath the surface of him, but he's managed to let people in despite it.

"You're a good person," I say.

"So are you."

chapter forty-two

The next day, Evan's finals are on a block schedule, so he's done at noon. He comes home to get me for my afternoon exams, essentially grabbing a quick snack then turning right around to drive me straight back to Ocean High, where he'll wait for me in the hallway. Three of my junior year curriculum classes required final papers instead of exams, but three more—US history, calculus, and English—have written tests that will be one hour each. Since my online school serves students throughout California, they've had multiple testing days and sites all week long based on subject. I could've spaced my finals out. I could've gone to three different locations on three different days this week, some of them hours away, but I decided once would be easier. For me.

However, the second my feet hit the concrete steps of the campus, I'm not sure I can stay.

"I shouldn't be here," I say.

"Just tell yourself you'll take the first one," Evan says. "And if worse comes to worst, you leave. But you have to at least try."

"You sound like Brenda."

He grins. "I sound like a psychologist with dreadlocks and tats? Cool."

I elbow his side. "No. You sound smart."

"I am smart."

I laugh. "Now you sound like Ben."

"Ben's smart, too."

"I know. I should have him take my finals for me."

Ocean High School is officially out for the summer, so the campus is empty. The whole time we're walking the hallways, Evan points stuff out to me. "That's the door to my science class." "Here's where I hang out at lunch." "A pregnant teacher fainted there."

By the time we arrive at the library, I realize he managed to keep me distracted the whole time we were walking through the school. We passed his dented locker and the musty gym. We passed the cafeteria, where the stench of day-old tater tots seeped through the doors and stuck to the nearby walls. And, because of Evan's constant play-by-play, not once did I picture Aaron Tiratore lurking around a corner.

In the hallway outside the library, Evan turns me to face him and rubs my shoulders like I'm a boxer about to enter the ring and he's loosening me up to fight. "You've got this," he says. I close my eyes and roll my neck back against his knuckles, trying to relax.

We stay like that for a few minutes until I pull away and nod my head at him like I'm ready. He fist-bumps me, then kisses my forehead. I leave him leaning against the wall with his thumbs hooked into the front pockets of his jeans. "I'll be right here when you're done."

I nod again and go inside.

Apparently I'm the first one to arrive, because the only other person here besides me is a portly but serious-looking man who must be the exam proctor. He's sitting on a stool at the counter where students go to check out books.

"Name?" he asks. His deep voice bounces off the empty walls of the library and settles in my stomach.

"Morgan Grant."

He checks a clipboard in front of him. "Got you. You can sign in here."

I walk over and scrawl my signature on a line next to my name. I notice there are only two other people on the list. And one of them has a first name I recognize from my live sessions. Blue. I guess his last name is Armstrong, because that's what's typed out next to *Blue*.

"You've gotta be kidding me," I mutter.

"What's that?"

"Nothing. Sorry." Of course there could be someone else named Blue, but what are the chances?

"Very well. The exams are closed notes, so you'll have to leave your bag up front with me."

"I don't have one." I hold my two pencils and two pens up. "Just this."

"Great, because that's all you'll need. Go ahead and grab a study carrel up front."

I take a seat in the one on the far right. I spread my pencils and pens out in front of me and stare at the chipping green paint and penis drawings graffitied onto the study carrel wall. I knot my fingers together and rest them on the edge of the table, rocking them back and forth.

Tick, tick, tick goes the clock on the wall behind me.

Let's get this over with.

The proctor coughs. It's ripe and phlegm-filled. He unwraps a cough drop and pops it into his mouth. I hear the click of it against his teeth.

It's too quiet in here.

I can detect everything.

The door to the library bangs open and I jump. A guy swaggers in. He has a blue-stained fauxhawk and cobalt Dr. Martens boots with loose laces, like he came here to see his favorite band. Not to take an exam.

"M'name's Blue. Where do you need me?"

The proctor clears his throat and motions him to sign in. Another girl arrives right after, and the proctor motions her over as well. The next thing I know, we're all settled into study carrels, and everyone is to the left of me because I planned it that way.

"You have sixty minutes and your time starts . . . now," the proctor says, hitting a button on his phone that I assume offers up some sort of sixty-minute countdown.

"Yo," Blue says to me as soon as we're supposed to be quiet. "You got an extra pencil? I only brought a pen." He holds it up to me. The black plastic top is flattened from his gnawing.

I turn away. I don't want to make eye contact. I don't want it to look like I'm cheating.

"Hey, hello? Pencil?"

I shake my head no, not looking up from my Scantron sheet even though staring at it so intently makes the letters and numbers go blurry.

"You have two of 'em. I can see the extra one on your desk."

I finally turn to face him. "I might need it," I hiss under my breath. "If something happens to the other one. I like to be prepared."

He smirks and turns to the girl on the other side of him. She hands over a pencil the first time he asks. I can feel him looking at me, like he wants me to know other people are less high-strung about sharing pencils. When I don't return the stare, he dives into his test, humming and tapping and being distracting the whole time.

We have a bathroom break in between tests. I walk out into the hallway, expecting that Evan might've left to wander around the school or breathe in fresh air outside. But he hasn't budged. He's sitting right there on the ground, listening to music and scrolling through his phone. He yanks his earbuds out of his ears when he sees me.

"Bathroom break," I explain.

"Here, I'll show you where," he says.

Blue watches us walk down the hallway. I can feel his eyes on my back. Maybe he recognized my name, too. Maybe he remembers antagonizing me in our live session. Maybe he gets off on screwing with people who like to be prepared.

Two more people join us for the second test. When that one is over, I stretch in the hallway. Blue wanders off to god knows where. The other girl who started with Blue and me never leaves the library.

Evan gives me a kiss before I head in to the last test. "Almost summer," he whispers.

I take my place at my study carrel and realize one of the two people who joined us for the second test is gone. The other one is still here. And the first girl. And Blue. Lucky me.

When the third exam is finally over, the proctor gives us a few minutes to go over our final answers. Blue leans back in his chair instead of double-checking his work. The front legs lift off the floor, but he uses the steel-toed tips of his boots to balance himself.

"Don't fall," I say.

He grins at me and pushes back on his chair again, like I've challenged him somehow. He rocks back farther, eyes on me the whole time. Farther and farther back he goes. I look down and see the chair is teetering on the very edges of its back legs now. He's grinning. Showing off. And then the chair topples backward, taking Blue with it. He hits the floor hard, and the force of his butt against the back of the chair makes it flip back over and land on his chest.

"Argh!" he bellows.

I try to hide a snicker in my armpit.

"Screw you," he says to me.

"You're an idiot." I get up, turn in my test, and step past Blue to get to the door. He stands there rubbing his chest and righting his chair. I can't get out of the library fast enough.

"Happy summer," Evan says, taking my hand as soon as he sees me.

"Happy summer." I kiss him. "Let's go."

We push through campus corridors and heavy doors. I think of the last day of school last year. I think of the sophomore hallway littered with loose-leaf papers torn free from notebooks. Of plans made for that night and the long, slow days ahead. Some of us had part-time jobs. Some of us planned to lounge on the sand from dusk until dawn while plugged in to music playlists. Some of us were traveling to see the other half of divorced parents who lived in other states, like Evan will do in August. None of us knew what would happen when we returned. Because it was before Aaron did what he did.

It was before everything changed.

This time, the last day of school is just a time stamp on how much I missed this year.

But now, there will be summer. And summer can be everything. Evan and I will surf and swim and smell like sunblock. In the evenings, we'll come back to Paradise Manor and jump in the pool to rinse off the sand and the stickiness. When it gets dark, we'll watch movies until Ben falls asleep, and then Evan and I will kiss each other until our lips get swollen.

chapter forty-three

When we get home, Evan only has a little bit of time to get ready for a celebratory last day of school dinner he's going to with his mom, aunt, and uncle. He knocks on my door on his way out. He's wearing jeans and a T-shirt so worn that it clings to him. It clings in a way that makes me want to ask him to stay.

"What're you gonna do tonight?" he asks as he hugs me against him. He smells like Evan. Like sunblock and surf wax even though he just took a shower. My own shirt rides up, and he presses his fingertips into the bare skin of my lower back, pulling me closer.

"Ben and I are going to watch a movie," I mumble into his clingy shirt. "Maybe pop popcorn. You know, summer stuff."

Evan leans down to kiss me goodbye. When his hands start to wander and he attempts to maneuver me back inside my apartment, I stop him.

"Don't you need to go?" I laugh. He pushes back on his heels, but steadies himself in front of me again. I give him a little push. "Go. Have fun."

He leans into me to bury his face against the crook of my neck, tightening his grip on my waist like he doesn't really want to leave. "Can we hang out when I get back?"

I grin. "Of course. We can hang out all summer long. Now go. Your mom never has any time off. Let her take you to dinner."

He straightens up, and his T-shirt seems even clingier since being pressed against me.

"What?" he asks, and I realize I'm staring at him all blown away by how cute he is.

"Nothing." I shift from one foot to the other. "Would it be bad if I told you to hurry home?"

"Morgan." He laughs. "If it were up to me, I'd already be back."

After Ben's bath, I encourage my mom to take the night off. She settles in her room with a book while Ben and I settle on the couch with a movie and a heaping bowl of popcorn. Ben tells me all about the last-day-of-school party they had in his classroom and the water balloon fight they had at his after-school day care.

"I got soaked." He snickers. "It went all the way through to my underwear."

"That's good stuff," I tell him.

He leans his head against my shoulder and props his bare feet up on the arm of the couch. I know he's just a little kid, but sometimes he looks so grown-up. Thankfully, my phone buzzes with a text before I start ugly-crying and telling my little brother to stop getting older.

Evan: *You up?*

Me: *What do you think? I live with a 6 y.o. who just started summer break.*

Evan: *LOL*

Me: *How's dinner?*

Evan: *Over. I miss u.*

My heart goes all fluttery. It's only three words, but the idea of being missed by Evan Kokua does something to me.

Me: *I miss you, too.*

Evan: *Can I come over now? I might have leftovers wrapped in tinfoil that looks like some sort of exotic animal.*

I laugh, and Ben asks me what's so funny. "Evan," I tell him.

"Yeah, Evan's funny all right." He chuckles to himself like Evan's sitting right here and just cracked a joke about dinosaur poop. He stretches, yawns, and curls up against me, his eyelids miraculously fluttering shut.

Me: *Come home. Ben is fading fast.*

Evan: *See u soon.*

Ben manages to fall asleep against my shoulder in the time I'm waiting for Evan to arrive. I pick him up and carry him to his bed. My phone vibrates with a text as soon as I've shut the door to our room.

Evan: *Can you come outside?*

I head to the front door and open it. Evan is standing there on my welcome mat. Waiting for me. Holding up his tinfoil-wrapped leftovers. "I think it's supposed to be a swan," he says, bending the long neck back into place as I take it in my hands.

"Fancy."

"We ate at a fancy restaurant."

"I didn't know Pacific Palms had one of those."

"I'll take you sometime."

I take a whiff through the tinfoil. "What's in here, anyway?"

"Come up to the roof and I'll show you."

"Oh, I bet you will."

"What? I just meant we'll have a picnic," he teases. "You have a dirty mind, Morgan Grant."

"You know you love it." I click the door shut behind me and take his hand. "I've never been on the roof. Aren't there opossums and other vermin up there?"

He pulls me around the corner. "I guess we'll find out."

"Super."

When we get to the edge of the building, Evan sets the leftovers on the ground and hammocks his hands together. "Climb on. I'll give you a boost." I look at the roof. It's only one story up, but it seems higher. "I've got you. Trust me."

I take a deep breath, stick my bare foot into his hands, and grab on to the storm drain, hoping I don't tear it down as he pushes me upward. Within seconds, I'm able to scramble across the worn wood shingles, though I'm certain I'm getting splinters and deadly brown recluse spider bites in the process.

I look down at Evan. "How will you get up here?"

He tosses the leftovers up to me and climbs onto the railing that wraps around the balcony of our floor. "Like this." He teeters on the thin metal like an adept tightrope walker.

"Oh, my god. I can't watch."

But before I can tear my eyes away, Evan jumps high enough to be able to grab the edge of Paradise Manor and hoist himself up and over. There's something to be said for being athletic. And agile. And Evan. He lands next to me with a thud and rolls over onto his back, staring up at the sky.

"Don't you dare let Ben ever see you do that."

He laughs, full and free, into the middle of the night. "Deal."

"Okay, let's check out these leftovers."

I begin to unwrap what has become a completely deformed tinfoil swan. I'm slow and deliberate, anticipating something good, but I start laughing when I see what's inside.

"You got a burger and fries at your fancy dinner?"

"What can I say? I'm a creature of habit."

"Bet they loved wrapping that one up." I take one of only two bites left of the burger and lie down next to Evan. I turn my head to look at him. "I know you didn't really bring me up here to eat a hamburger."

"Are you saying offering you the remnants of my cold food isn't as smooth as I think it is?"

"You don't have to have smooth moves to get me to hang out with you."

"Oh, thank god." He rolls over and hooks one of his knees between mine, presses his mouth to my lips, and trails his fingertips along the hem of my shirt.

And then there's just the dark.

And the stars.

And the air.

And us.

chapter forty-four

The first day of summer vacation roars to a start. By nine a.m., the sun is blazing hot enough to heat my apartment to an unbearable degree. Evan and I decide to haul Ben, his boogie board, and Evan's surfboard down to the beach after I've packed sandwiches and smothered my brother in SPF 50.

I decide today is as good a day as any to practice my driving, and I find parking easily because I head to the strip of beach where the tourists don't go. I realize this means we'll probably see people I know, but I'm hoping we can set up camp on the outskirts. I'd like to take my baby steps without the whole world watching. And since nobody is expecting to see us, they might not even recognize me.

It's surprising when the feel of the sand squishing between my toes nearly makes me weep. I've missed it in a good way. Because I'm a person who belongs at the beach. By locking myself up in my apartment, I've been denying who I am. I need sand and salt water. Sunblock and string bikinis. Sun and sanity.

We lay our striped towels down, three in a row, and Ben takes off for the ocean. He's a pretty good swimmer, but he needs supervision because he has no fear. I follow him out, and when the water licks at my toes, I know I'm home.

Really and truly home.

I pull Ben up on my waist and take him out to where the waves are breaking. I grip the soft sand below with my toes and sink my heels in to brace myself against the salty spray coming at us. And then I tell Ben to hold his breath before we duck under to swim out past the break.

It's perfect here, with the cool water all around us and my favorite kid in the world hanging on my back. Absolutely perfect. Ben lets go of me and swims in circles around me, sometimes stopping to tread water and catch his breath.

After a while, we come back in from the ocean. I settle on my striped towel, put on my sunglasses, and wring salty water from my hair. Evan heads to the water with his surfboard. I zone out, staring at the ocean, while Ben attempts to dig a hole to China with a miniature shovel. I soon notice three figures slicing through the water in the distance. Their swim strokes are perfectly in sync, strong and seasoned, plowing against the current in bright orange swim caps like they know exactly what they're doing. Watching them makes me want to swim, too. Really swim. I don't mean going back and forth in the fifteen-yard kiddie pool in the courtyard of Paradise Manor. I mean tearing through the vast open ocean. As the swimmers get closer, I see they're wearing PPHS caps. They're from my swim team. Or my old swim team. I don't know what to call it anymore.

They pop up to tread water, and one of them points to the shore. They change direction, heading for the sand. I'm not surprised they've chosen to stop here. This is where people from PPHS hang out. But I kind of hope I don't know them. Which is crazy to hope for, because whoever it is was on my swim team. Two of the swimmers catch a good wave that takes them all the way in and spits them out in the white wash. The third one catches another wave. They all stumble out of the ocean, wobbling on their noodly sea legs as they hit firm ground again. When they tear off their goggles and swim caps, I recognize Chelsea and Brianna right away. And then I recognize Taylor, too. I don't know when they all got to be so tight, but they're definitely taking their swim training seriously.

I hope my sunglasses are big enough to hide me.

"No way!" Chelsea shouts when she gets close enough to see I'm here. "Brianna! It's Morgan."

My sunglasses aren't big enough to hide me.

The two of them run up and topple me over in a salty hug. I feel like I'm being attacked by wet puppies. Their enthusiasm for seeing me is overwhelming. And touching, too. I assumed they'd stopped missing me.

Taylor ambles up behind them. I swear she's even buffer than the last time I saw her, but I might just be making that up in my head now. She wrings out her thick braid as well as she can and pushes it back over her shoulder, where it lands with a thump. She ruffles Ben's sandy head of hair and plops down on the ground next to me. Brianna and Chelsea have taken up residence on my towel.

"It's so good to see you," Brianna trills as Chelsea hugs me to her, nodding emphatically.

"Just in time for summer," Taylor says, and smiles at me. "We're training to swim the Pacific Palms Rough Water in August. You should join us."

"I don't think I'm badass enough," I say.

Taylor ticks her gaze at Evan bobbing around in the ocean on his surfboard. "Someone thinks you are."

"Seriously. Who's the hot dude?" Brianna asks.

"He's my next-door neighbor."

"Wish I had a next-door neighbor like that," Chelsea says.

Taylor grins. "He's more than a neighbor."

"Ooh. Do tell," Chelsea says, rubbing her hands together.

Taylor sits back and gives my friends the scoop on Evan Kokua. And, like that, we're just four girls sitting on the beach, talking about boys, the same as we did last summer. I realize all is forgiven if I want it to be. Because that's what real friends do. Even new friends like Taylor do that. And maybe we could be even better friends because of what happened. Because there's an unspoken understanding between us, and that's probably how it is with everyone who was at school the day Aaron Tiratore did what he did. I just haven't been around my former classmates enough to know it. I've been living with this gripping fear that doesn't ever really let go. But surely Taylor, Brianna, and Chelsea feel it, too.

"Do you guys ever get scared?" I blurt out.

"Are you kidding? Every day of my life, I remember I could've died," Taylor says as she straightens out the straps on her bikini and shifts in the sand. "But what good does that do me or anyone else who survived that day? Or the ones who didn't? Aren't we doing everyone who died a disservice if we don't say screw it and live? We have to live because they can't. We have to live as hard as we can, not half-assed, but all the way. We owe them that."

"Live, Morgan!" Chelsea hollers. "Say you'll train with us!"

"I'll think about it."

Brianna hugs me to her. "Bullshit. You're so in."

I wish I could be as sure as she is.

Once we've rinsed off all the sand from the beach, I leave Evan and Ben in the pool to practice underwater somersaults and handstands in the shallow end.

"I've gotta make a phone call," I say, scampering up the stairs.

I settle on the top step and dial a number I know by heart. Sage answers on the first ring. I can tell she doesn't recognize Evan's random Hawaii number because she says hello with a question mark at the end of it.

"It's me," I say.

"Where are you?"

"Pacific Palms. Someone else's phone."

"Ah."

"I miss you."

She pauses. Quiet. Contemplating.

"I just wanted to get right to it," I say.

"It's okay. I miss you, too."

"I'm sorry."

"I know. Me too."

"I was just trying to deal, you know? And I realize I was really selfish in my dealing—"

"Morgan," she cuts me off. "I understand. We all had to get through it in our own way. I'm still working on it."

"Me too."

"Tell me how."

So I do. I settle sideways on the top stair, lean my back against the wall, and tell Sage everything. I tell her about Brenda and my apartment. I tell her about Ben's play and the backpack fiasco. And then I tell her how I gave Aaron a ride to school. She sucks in a breath when I get to that part.

"You could've told me," she says. "You could've trusted me."

I try to explain. "I didn't trust myself."

"But you know it's not your fault, right?"

"I know that now."

"God, I'm so sorry, Morgan. I wish you would've let me be there for you."

"I didn't deserve to have you there for me. I failed you as a friend. I wasn't there for you when you needed me."

"I'd be lying if I didn't say it hurt. But I get it now."

"Really?"

"Really."

"So we're okay?"

She laughs like I told her a joke. "Of course! I was just waiting for you to call. I've been sitting by the phone in the most pathetic way possible."

"Why didn't you call me?"

"I knew I needed to let you make the first move."

"Always playing hard to get."

The two of us trail off into peals of laughter. I can picture her on the other end of the line, trying to catch her breath. Sage has the best laugh. I've missed it.

chapter forty-five

Brenda and I decided to make our once-a-week meetings on Tuesdays, so almost a whole week of summer passes before our first session. Evan offers to watch Ben so I can drive to Brenda's two-story office building in the middle of town. As I make my way up the stairs, I remember the last time I was here. It took every ounce of energy I had to get through the front door, even with my mom right next to me.

Today, I push through the entrance and, when I step onto the plush green carpet of the waiting room, I feel relief. There are two chairs and a sign on another closed door in front of me that says Brenda's with a patient. I settle into a chair to wait, listening to the whir of the air conditioner and thumbing through an outdated travel magazine.

Five minutes later, when the door swings open, a girl who looks my age walks out with Brenda right behind her. Brenda smiles hello to me as the girl hustles out of the front door, like she's in a hurry to leave.

I get it. This stuff is private. She doesn't need to make small talk with me.

"Shall we?" Brenda asks.

I nod and follow her inside her office.

"So," Brenda says as we settle into chairs across from each other. "We're here. How do you feel?"

"Accomplished?" I say it like a question, like I need confirmation.

"Yes. Certainly. This *is* an accomplishment." She smiles at me. "Tell me about your summer so far."

I do. I tell her about beach chairs and boardwalks. Sleeping in and swimming laps. Pancakes and passing time. Ben and Evan. Evan and me. My mom.

My friends.

"I saw Chelsea and Brianna," I say. "I called Sage." The words come out in a rush. I realize I'm excited about them.

"How did that go?"

"It was good. It was *normal*."

Brenda smiles. "How so?"

"I thought it would be so hard but it was really okay. It's like they'll always be my friends no matter what. And I'll always be theirs."

"Exactly. I'm so glad you've reconnected, Morgan. It's important. For all of you."

I look past Brenda's shoulder and through the window at the bright blue sky and green trees outside.

"I can almost see PPHS," I say. "Did you know it's opening again in the fall?"

"I did. How do you feel about that?"

"I want to go back. I miss it."

"What do you miss about it?"

I laugh. "The thing I miss most is what scares me the most: all the people. I'm sick of taking classes by myself on a computer. I miss literature discussions, swim team, and eating lunch with my friends."

Brenda nods. "Those are good things to miss. I'm so happy to hear you want to return." She's looking me right in the eye and grinning so wide that I can see the gap between her front teeth.

"It'll be hard," I say.

"You can do it."

I believe her. I have to. Because right now, more than anything, I don't want my senior year to be like my junior year. I want to walk the hallways of Pacific Palms High School when it opens again in the fall, no matter how hard it seems.

Chelsea and Brianna will be there. And Evan. And Taylor. The memories will be there, too. Along with a new building and a memorial wall.

"What else is on your mind?" she asks.

"I have a letter here. For my dad."

Brenda sits up straight. "Do you want to share it?"

I pick at some blue nail polish flaking off my pinky finger. "I don't want to read it out loud. Can you just take a look?"

She holds her hand out for the letter. I fish it out of the pocket of my shorts and pass it over. She pulls the letter from the envelope I've addressed to my dad at his rehab facility and unfolds the crinkled paper.

"It's short," she notes.

"Yeah. But it says everything."

> *Dear Dad,*
>
> *I know you might be embarrassed about things you've done, but I want you to know I understand them, in a way. Because I've lived them, too. I understand what it*

feels like to think you've disappointed people you love. But
the thing is, when people love you, they love you no
matter what. I realize this now.

I've always loved you. Even when it hurt. Even when
you weren't around. Even when I worried you'd forgotten
who I am. I've always loved you.

I would like to find a way to have you in my life again
because I miss you.

Love,
Morgan

"You're right," Brenda says, folding the letter back into the envelope and handing it over to me. "That's all that needed to be said. Do you feel good about it?"

"Yes. But would it be stupid to send it to him?"

"Why would that be stupid?"

"What if he doesn't want it?"

"I think he'll want it. He wouldn't have checked into rehab if he didn't want to repair mistakes he's made. And maybe, even though he's the adult, you might need to be the one to reach out first." Brenda taps her pen against her notepad.

I think of Sage and how I reached out to her first. I don't regret doing it. "Okay."

"Now that I think of it, there's a mailbox at the end of the block. What do you say we send your letter off right now?"

"Right now right now?"

"Sure. Why not?"

I adjust my ponytail, nod, and stand up. Brenda grabs her keys and sunglasses, and I follow her through the front door.

Down the stairs.

Around the corner.

Across the sidewalk.

To the mailbox in the distance.

When we get there, I pull on the big blue handle and toss my letter inside. I don't hesitate. I just let it go.

acknowledgments

Heartfelt thanks and gratitude go out to so many people who cheered me on and helped me out while I made this book a book.

To the entire FSG/Macmillan team, especially my editor, Joy Peskin, for seeing what was on the page and also what wasn't. Thank you for loving these characters as much as I do, talking about them like real people, and for helping Morgan's story grow the layers it needed. Your brilliance, guidance, and kindness are a debut author's dream and I am so fortunate to get to work with you. To Andrew Arnold who made a book cover that literally made me gasp with excitement when I first saw it. It is perfect. To my keen-eyed copy-editors, Cynthia Ritter and Kate Hurley as well as Karen Ninnis, thank you for your patience and support in getting this just right. And to the lovely Angie Chen plus everyone else behind the scenes at FSG, I am so grateful for you. Additional thanks to the Macmillan UK Children's team, especially Venetia Gosling, whose enthusiasm for *Underwater* means the world to me.

To my superagent, Kate Schafer Testerman, who discovered Morgan in the slush pile and changed my life with a phone call that has gone down in history as one of the best phone calls of my entire life. You are my dream agent and I am so very lucky to know you. Thank you to the whole kt literary family, including Renee Nyen, Sara Megibow, and my fellow authors. I am humbled to be in your company. And extra thanks to Amy Spalding who took me to lunch and made me feel like an official agency sibling from day one.

Jon and Kai, my two favorite people in the whole world, thank you for every sacrifice you've made and for always believing in this dream of mine. You are the reason for everything and I love you both so much. For my mom, who I think might be the only person more excited about *Underwater* than I am, thank you for encouraging me when I wanted to major in creative writing and then go on to grad school to write some more. I love you. To Michael, Liane, and Julia for never doubting, even when it was taking a really long time to get here. And finally to my dad who told me the best stories about walking in the woods when I was a kid. I miss you every day.

Elise Robins and Stacy Wise, my loyal SHC, this book is what it is because of you. Thank you for being there through every up, down, and freak-out

(I know I have a lot of them). Straight-up fist bump to both of you. And to my beta readers, Lisa Pak, Dave Carpenter, Heidi Swan, and the genius writer/#1 funny, Mariano Svidler, thank you for asking all the right questions.

To my early readers, Carli, Jill, Jenny F., Louisa, Katie, Jenny M., and Missy. You all read *Underwater* because you love books. I'm so glad you loved *my* book.

To Robynne, thank you for being kind enough to help me with Morgan's therapy and being there to answer questions before, during, and after writing. And to my cousin, Johnny Boy Matherne, thank you for sharing details of your US Army experience with me. Your expertise goes beyond measure and any mistakes contained in these pages are mine and mine alone.

To my best friend since high school, Julie Laing, thank you for letting me write stories on your computer and for supporting everything I've written since tenth grade. I love you more. And to my other best friend and amazing writer, Brooke Hodess, thank you for giving me a second chance even after I gave you my BRF on the USC tram. I love you (and Hedwig) always.

To my HB cheering section: Dina, Geri, Jane, Michelle, Molly, Brooke B., Carol, Elizabeth, and Kelly. I am so lucky to have you in my life. Additional cheering from Ken Baker, Gus Mastrapa, and Patrick Sauer is very much appreciated. And to my aunt, Dr. Beverly Matherne, thank you for making me feel like a real writer since high school.

To Shannon Parker, I have such mad respect for you and your writing talent. Thank you for your love, your friendship, your amazing critique notes, and an immediate response to any crisis. I don't know what I'd do without you.

A shout out to my loyal Young Adultish blog fans, thank you for always making me feel extraordinary.

To The Sweet Sixteens team, especially my fellow administrators, I'm so honored to take this journey with you. And to the Sixteen to Read crew, thank you for being so supportive and clever.

Last but not least, thank you to the people who didn't roll their eyes when I said I was writing a book. And didn't roll their eyes again when I said I was writing another one. And didn't roll their eyes again when I said I was writing another one. The road to publication is about perseverance and you were the first people to say, "We knew you could do it!" when it finally happened. You have no idea how much that unwavering support kept me going.